Also by Susanna Shore

House of Magic
Hexing the Ex
Saved by the Spell

P.I. Tracy Hayes
Tracy Hayes, Apprentice P.I.
Tracy Hayes, P.I. and Proud
Tracy Hayes, P.I. to the Rescue
Tracy Hayes, P.I. with the Eye
Tracy Hayes, from P.I. with Love
Tracy Hayes, Tenacious P.I.
Tracy Hayes, Valentine of a P.I.
Tracy Hayes, P.I. on the Scent

Two-Natured London
The Wolf's Call
Warrior's Heart
A Wolf of Her Own
Her Warrior for Eternity
A Warrior for a Wolf
Magic under the Witching Moon
Moonlight, Magic and Mistletoes
Crimson Warrior
Magic on the Highland Moor
Wolf Moon

Thrillers
Personal
The Assassin

Hexing the Ex

House of Magic 1

Susanna Shore

Crimson House Books

Hexing the Ex
Copyright © 2021 A. K. S. Keinänen
All rights reserved.

The moral right of the author has been asserted.

No part of this book may be reproduced, translated, or distributed without permission, except for brief quotations in critical articles and reviews.

This is a work of fiction. Names, characters, places, dialogues and incidents either are the product of the author's imagination or are used fictitiously. Any resemblance to actual events, organizations or persons, living or dead, except those in public domain, is entirely coincidental.

Book Design: A. K. S. Keinänen
Cover Design: A. K. S. Keinänen
Cover Image: Sergey Myakishev

ISBN 978-952-7061-45-9 (paperback edition)
ISBN 978-952-7061-44-2 (e-book edition)

www.susannashore.com

One

I'M NOT ONE FOR PREMONITIONS. I don't interpret every shiver in my spine as a portent, and I don't believe my Aunt Clara's bones when she declares that they predict doom. She just picks a random news item and announces that her bones knew it was going to happen.

But when my sandals sank into a soaked carpet as I stepped onto the small landing outside my flat, I knew everything was not well inside.

My second clue was the flood of water that flushed over my ankles when I opened the door.

Oh, bugger.

I abandoned the luggage I'd laboriously dragged up the steep stairs to the third floor, and crossed the small foyer in a couple of soggy leaps to the bathroom where I could hear the water running. I yanked the door open and got my feet washed a second time.

The sight inside turned my bones liquid, but I stiffened my spine and waded through the water to the running shower and the prone figure lying under it—on the drain.

"Nick!"

I kneeled by him and was instantly drenched by the shower. "Bloody hell!"

Sputtering, I reached blindly for the faucet and turned it off before focusing on my flatmate again. I lifted his head that was mercifully wedged in the corner so that it was above the water, and patted his cheeks. He was breathing, but completely out of it.

My temper flared now that I knew he was alive. "You bloody dope-head! What have I told you about showering when coming down from your high?"

He'd passed out in the shower before, but he'd never caused such a flood. Mostly because I'd been home and had been able to prevent disaster. But I'd been away on a holiday for two weeks, foolishly thinking that I could trust him not to wreck the place while I was gone.

I tried to take a hold under his arms, but his slack body was surprisingly heavy, and his wet skin was slippery. Getting up, I wrapped my hands around his wrists and pulled, which worked better. The drain finally open, the water began to surge down with a deep gurgle.

Sliding and gliding on the wet bathroom tiles, I dragged Nick to the hallway. The wall-to-wall carpet was soaked, but he was wet anyway, so I just dropped him there. His spread-eagled lanky form revealed details of his anatomy I really didn't want to see but—sadly—had witnessed before.

Then I fetched my luggage from the landing, carried it to my room that was miraculously dry, and stripped to my underwear. I'd soon be sweaty cleaning the mess Nick had made, so there was no point wearing clothes. Then I headed to the bathroom and got to work.

Happy homecoming, Phoebe. Happy fricking homecoming.

Hexing the Ex

~ ~ ~

I HADN'T PLANNED ON spending the last day of my holiday getting sloshed in the pub down the street, but then again, I hadn't planned spending it sloshing in the bathroom either. So here I was.

Nick was keeping me company, looking suitably sheepish and paying for our drinks. He'd woken up midway through my cleaning operation and offered to help, but he'd been completely useless, so I'd sent him to his bedroom and ordered him to stay there until further notice. Luckily for my blood pressure, he'd complied.

"We will be evicted. You know that, right?" I told him gloomily, staring at the golden liquid in my glass with unseeing eyes.

He made to reach for my hand, but thought the better of it. "You don't know that for sure."

I lifted my gaze to his baby blues that so well fit his personality. "We flooded the flat downstairs. I'd say that's cause enough for evicting us."

Mrs Keating had manifested at our open doorway as I'd been ineffectually trying to sop up the water from the carpet in the foyer with all the towels I could find, yelling and threatening us with consequences for ruining her home. The only reason our landlord hadn't shown up too was because it was Sunday and he couldn't be bothered.

Nick's shoulders slumped, but only briefly. "I'll move in with Betty," he declared happily, impervious to the sardonic brow I cocked in response.

"And what if she doesn't want you to live with her?"

I wouldn't have lived with him if I could've afforded a place in central London on my own. If I were his girlfriend, I'd keep him away from my home.

Then again, I wouldn't have dated him in the first place. He was fun company and nice to look at when clothed, with dishevelled, lanky charm, but a sporadically-employed actor with a propensity for recreational drug use wasn't what I was looking for in a boyfriend.

"Why wouldn't she?"

He sounded genuinely surprised and likely was. He was one of those people who trusted life to carry him, and reality to bend to his needs. And it did, amazingly often.

I took a sip from my pint to keep my thoughts to myself. "We'll still need money to pay for the repairs."

I hadn't caused the damage, but Nick never had any money to speak of, on top of which it was my name on the lease. I'd end up paying. I had insurance, but I doubted it would cover this. There was likely a clause that ruled passing out in the shower as deliberate damage.

He stretched languidly and then ran fingers through his overgrown, chestnut hair. "Can't you ask money from your parents?"

The mere thought brought bile to my mouth. It wasn't that we didn't get along. I'd just spent two weeks in their villa in Southern France and I'd had great time. It was what they would want in exchange for the money. Namely, that I get married and take my place as the family representative in society. The topic had come up often enough—again—during my visit.

I wasn't against marriage, per se. I resented that they thought it was the only thing I was good for. But they'd been fairly old when they had me, and belonged to a world where women didn't really exist outside the home.

"Not if I can help it," I stated. Which I likely couldn't, but I'd worry about that later. "But I'll still need a new home, and I don't have a handy boyfriend to move in with."

Nick frowned, puzzled. "What happened to what's his name?"

"Troy. We broke up two months ago." And even if we'd been together, he wouldn't have been my first choice for help.

"Huh?"

I heroically refrained from reminding him that I'd told him about it at the time, and several times since. Or ranted, more like. Nothing brushes a girl's ego like learning that the man she's been dating for over a year thinks that an assistant to an art and antiques dealer isn't quite as good as a corporate lawyer for a girlfriend, but since said assistant is from an influential family, he's been dating her too, just in case her family could give him the boost to greatness he believes he deserves.

I gave him a boost, all right.

Nick finished his beer and got up. "I'd best head to Betty's immediately."

"Shouldn't you call first?" I asked, alarmed, but he grinned.

"And give her a chance to say no? I don't think so. It's much better to show up at her door with a duffel bag and look so pitiful she has to take me in."

That was one way to handle it. Unfortunately, I didn't have anyone that I could look pitiful in front of for a place to stay. The thought of a sofa in someone's already crowded flat didn't exactly fill me with excitement either. I was twenty-six. I needed a door I could close behind me when I went to bed.

Nick pecked a kiss on my cheek and disappeared into the crowd filling the pub. I had a funny feeling I'd never see him again and a brief panic flared, but I stifled it mercilessly. We'd been flatmates for two years, during which I'd paid the full rent more often than I cared to remember, filled the fridge too regularly for my finances, constantly cleaned the house after him, and as a crowning achievement had been evicted because of him—or would be, in any case. Let others take care of him from now on.

I finished my drink in a more leisurely pace, but I didn't feel like staying in the pub alone, so I left too. I paused outside the pub and wondered what I should do next. It wasn't even nine yet, but I was knackered. I'd caught an early flight from Nice to Paris that morning, taken the Eurostar to London, and then dealt with the disaster back home. And I would have to wake up early for work the next day.

But I was in no hurry to return to a flat that smelled of wet dog and sloshed under my feet. So I found myself strolling down the high street in the opposite direction. There were plenty of people around, standing outside the pubs with their pints or heading from one pub to another, but the side streets were emptier. I knew better than take one of them after dark, so I settled with checking the wares on shop windows with no real interest in them.

Clerkenwell, northeast of the City's erstwhile walls, was a trendy neighbourhood and pretty expensive too, even if the older buildings like mine on St. John Street weren't always in first-rate repair. I could never find a new place here with what I paid for the current one. If I even could find a place. London had a huge housing problem. People fought for closet converts and paid twice for them what I paid now.

What if I ended up homeless?

Hexing the Ex

A painful knot in my stomach threatened to push the beer up as I imagined the bleakness of my future. I could always ask my parents for help, but even they couldn't conjure flats out of thin air. The house in Wimbledon I'd grown up in had been sold when they moved to France, so that wasn't an option anymore, and I'd die before I went to live with any of my relatives. Aunt Clara's granddaughter, Olivia, was my age, but we weren't close. I doubted she was willing to share her Chelsea flat with me.

Tears clouded my eyes and I blinked furiously to clear them. I glanced around to see if anyone had noticed, and my attention was caught by a small shop across the street with the lights still on. It was warm and yellow and spilled on the pavement like an invitation. Needing a distraction from my woes, I crossed the street to take a closer look.

The shop was narrow, only the width of one bay window and the door, and almost disappeared between two larger ones, which probably was why I had never noticed it before. A small round table and two chairs were placed in the window, like in a café or tearoom. It looked inviting.

Curious, I peered in, and saw a couple of more tables, but it didn't look like a café; it looked like a bookshop maybe. There were low hardwood shelves circling the room, books on one wall, tea in large tin jars on another, and all sorts of knickknacks on the last one by the counter at the back.

It looked like it had been here forever. I scanned the window and the door for the name of the place, but they were bare. Instead, my eyes landed on a white placard at the bottom corner of the window: Room to let. Inquire inside.

My heart jumped. Could this be the answer to my problem?

I tried to quench my enthusiasm. Likely the room had gone already and they'd just forgotten to take off the sign. But it wouldn't hurt to ask.

As I reached for the door handle, a delicious tingle ran down my spine. I wasn't one for premonitions, but I had a really good feeling about this.

Two

A SMALL BELL ABOVE THE DOOR chimed as I entered. A couple of low steps led up, made of mahogany like the floor and the shelves. I climbed them to the shop and was instantly surrounded by a multitude of scents. Not overwhelming; more like a carefully composed bouquet that didn't irritate my nose. I glanced around and located several scent sticks here and there.

A woman appeared from the backroom. She was maybe in her late thirties or very early forties, and tall, with the kind of narrow body that looked great in the black skinny jeans and spaghetti-strapped top she was wearing. Her short hair was a shock of red curls that looked natural, and were so thick that the glasses she'd lifted on her head practically disappeared in them.

I crossed the floor to her, taking a casual look at the wares on the shelf next to her—and then looked again. There were tarot cards, healing stones and crystals, small glass vials filled with colourful liquids, and mysterious items I couldn't immediately identify.

"Is this a witch's shop?" I blurted out, delighted, instead of what I was supposed to ask, which was about the room. "I've never been to one." I didn't really believe in such nonsense, but each to their own.

The woman smiled. Her face was narrow, with pronounced cheekbones, straight brows and sharp freckled nose. Her eyes were light blue, and her smile made them twinkle. "Yes, it is."

"Are you a witch? Because you don't look like one."

She tilted her head. "And you don't look like our usual clientele, so I presume you're here for the room?"

I glanced at my white linen trousers and pink tank-top, both slightly wrinkled, as I'd pulled them from my luggage for the pub. Pink toenails peered out of pink flip-flops. Maybe witches only wore black.

I nodded in answer to her question, holding my breath. "Is it still available?"

"It is," she assured me. "I only put the sign there half an hour ago."

Imagine my luck. I didn't usually walk in this direction, and the one time I did I came across exactly what I needed.

"Would I do?"

I straightened and looked at her expectantly. I hadn't exactly dressed for a house interview, and my long cinnamon brown hair was in a careless bun, because I hadn't had the energy to wash it after the clean-up operation.

"I'm twenty-six, I have a good job and good credit."

The woman's smiled deepened. "And what's your name?"

"Oh, it's Phoebe. Phoebe Thorpe."

She offered me her hand and I shook it. "I'm Amber Boyle. Why don't we check the room first in case it's not to your liking?"

I grimaced. "I'm facing eviction, so trust me, I'll like it."

Amber cocked an inquisitive brow and I realised I shouldn't have told her that. For one, it made me look desperate and she might up the rent on the fly; for another, it made me seem like an undesirable tenant.

"My flatmate wrecked the place while I was on holiday," I explained hastily. I wasn't above throwing Nick under the proverbial bus. Besides, it was true.

She shook her head but didn't comment, and I tried not to read anything to it. "Let me call Luca to man the shop first."

She disappeared into the backroom and hollered to what from my angle looked like the cellar. A moment later a man about my age entered the shop. He was only slightly taller than my five seven, and tightly muscled, with sandy hair in a short ponytail, angular face, and an appreciative smile as he checked me out, his green eyes lingering at my cleavage. It was good cleavage.

"Luca Marlow here has the basement flat, and he helps in the shop at nights," Amber told me. "Phoebe Thorpe is here for the empty room."

Luca offered me a hand to shake. "Welcome to House of Magic."

"I haven't been accepted yet," I said hastily as I shook it, fearing he'd jinxed my chances, but he grinned.

"You found here, didn't you?"

The comment baffled me, but before I had a chance to ask what he meant, Amber led me down a short hallway that ended at the door to the back yard. We didn't go out, but through an inner door on the left to a staircase up that ended at a similar short hallway. It was painted in elegant grey, with white skirting boards, and had a polished hardwood floor. Hooks for coats and racks for shoes lined the wall opposite the stairs. At the end of the hallway, the stairs continued up, and a narrow window offered a view to the back yard and the buildings on the street over.

Amber herded me to the opposite direction, to an open kitchen and living room that were separated by a sturdy oaken dining table that seated at least ten and doubled as a kitchen worktop. The room was only as wide as the shop below, maybe six metres, with two narrower bay windows towards the street. The living room furniture was stuffed Victorian sofas in red and green, glossy occasional tables, and tasselled lampshades, all genuine items at first glance. It was overflowing and utterly charming.

A short and plump woman in an ankle-length peasant skirt and a T-shirt was kneading bread dough by the table. She turned to look when we entered.

"Giselle, this is Phoebe Thorpe for the empty room. Phoebe, this is my wife, Giselle Lynn."

She was about Amber's age, with steel-grey hair in a fetching pixie cut, soft features with deep dimples, and large chocolate brown eyes that crinkled at the corners when she smiled. She showed her hands that were covered with dough.

"Welcome, Phoebe. I'll refrain from shaking your hand if you don't mind."

I assured her it was fine. "Your home looks lovely."

"Thank you," she said, her smile deepening. "I inherited most of the furniture from my aunt with the house. It's too much of a hassle to carry them down those stairs, so it's good we like them."

I could imagine.

Amber gestured at the kitchen. "Breakfast is self-serve, but if you show up around seven, Gis will make you a proper English breakfast. Dinner is at six, but if you can't make it, there are usually plenty of leftovers you can heat."

My mouth dropped open. "The rent includes food?"

Giselle shrugged. "It didn't at first, but it makes the place feel more like our home and not a half-way house when we all gather to eat together."

"You're also welcome to join us here to watch TV or whatever. If we want to be alone, we'll stay on our floor, which is the next one," Amber added. She headed back to the hallway and we took the stairs up.

"Gis and I have our bedroom, bath, and study here," she explained at the next floor, but we continued up. I had a quick impression of similar dark grey walls and white skirting boards as the floor below.

The top floor was like the others, fairly narrow and deep. It had been divided to two rooms, with a bathroom in the hallway. Amber gave me a peek there, and while it wasn't terribly large, it was recently refurbished in a retro style, clean and pretty.

She opened the door on the right. "This is your room. I hope you don't mind that it's furnished."

Since I didn't own the furniture in my flat, I definitely didn't mind. Besides, the room looked nice. Walls were covered with old-rose wallpaper, and the floor with soft, dark grey carpet. It was barely wide enough for the double bed to fit sideways under the window, but it was deep enough for a large hardwood wardrobe and a drawer, a desk, bookshelf, and an armchair upholstered in old-rose fabric. It looked like it was made for me.

A grey cat was stretched on the rose bedspread like a living dot on the i. Emerald green eyes turned to study us, slightly affronted for the intrusion.

"That's Griselda. She thinks she owns the place," Amber said with a fond smile. "I hope you're not allergic to cats, because she's impossible to keep away from the bedrooms. She always finds a way in."

"I love cats," I assured her, going to the bed to pet her, which she graciously allowed. "She's lovely. And the room is perfect."

Amber smiled. "And it has a broadband connection too. When can you move in?"

I startled. "Don't you intend to interview anyone else?" I held my breath until she shook her head.

"You saw the sign."

I still didn't know what that meant, but I wasn't about to ask in case it made her change her mind. "So how much is it for a month?"

I hoped it wasn't beyond my means, but I already loved the place and would beg for my parents for a monthly allowance if I couldn't afford it otherwise. But she named a sum that was pretty much what I currently paid.

"Plus the food and utilities, right?" I asked.

"No, those are included." She returned to the hallway before I managed to voice my bafflement, and pointed at the other door. "Ashley is a firefighter and currently on a twenty-four-hour shift, but you'll meet eventually."

She headed back down the stairs and I hurried after her. "Can I move in tonight?"

She shot an amused look over her shoulder. "Of course. The shop's open past midnight anyway, so it's not like you'll disturb anyone. Do you need help?"

I gave it a thought. "I'll fetch some clothes and toiletries tonight, and the rest over the weekend. There are some books that'll be heavier, but otherwise I only have clothes to move."

Even the kitchenware belonged to the flat, and those that didn't, I would leave behind.

We returned to the kitchen, where Giselle had put the bread in the oven. Delicious scents were starting to fill the room.

"Here's the lease," she said. It had my name already on it, as if she'd been sure that I would be accepted. "Read it carefully and return it in the morning."

I was given a key to the back door, and then I followed Amber to the shop, where Luca greeted me with a delighted smile. "I knew you'd stay. No one can resist Gis's food."

I hadn't even tasted it, but the idea of not having to cook for myself was immensely appealing.

I hurried the half a mile to my flat that smelled even worse now. I emptied the fridge of perishables, a quick job as I'd done it before I went on holiday and Nick hadn't filled it again. Then I selected a week's worth of clothes and put them in a garment bag, and threw underwear and other necessities into a backpack along with my laptop. That left no room for shoes, so I needed another bag for those.

Thus burdened, I made the short journey back to my new home, excitement carrying my steps where earlier they'd been heavy. I couldn't believe my luck, and half expected the shop to have disappeared while I was gone.

But it was still there. My heart skipped a beat when the warmly-lit window came to a view.

A man exited the shop just then, briefly illuminated by the light, and I halted in surprise. Was that my boss?

This wasn't exactly a neighbourhood where Archibald Kane, the owner of Kane's Arts and Antiques, usually hung out in. He lived in the luxurious Belgravia on the west side of central London, and handled his social life there too, as far as I knew. We were barely on a first-name basis—I called him Kane though, on his insistence—so I didn't know about his private life. He loved curious items, but the wares in the shop weren't anything he usually set his sights in. They couldn't be the lure.

Maybe it wasn't him. London was full of thirty-something, tall and leanly muscled men in tailor-made black suits, some of them even with aristocratic noses and thick black hair that billowed lightly as if a private wind were constantly blowing it.

I had to be sure.

He turned a corner and I practically ran to cross the street after him. My bags and flip-flops slowed me down, and when I turned to the one-lane street, it was empty.

My curiosity stronger than my sense of caution, I hurried down the short lane to the next corner and peeked around it. And there he was. But he wasn't alone anymore.

He was facing a much shorter man in a tweed jacket that didn't close over his potbelly. It was dark and the streetlight didn't allow me to see his face clearly, but the short man was angry. He was gesticulating wildly, and then he poked my boss in the chest with a stubby finger.

A huge mistake, if he was Kane.

The man definitely pulled himself straight like Kane in a mood, his hair billowing even more wildly than usually, as if powered by his anger.

Hexing the Ex

The older man cowered instantly, but it was too late. There was a flash of bright light that forced me to close my eyes, and a boom that I more felt than heard. When I opened my eyes again, the older man was lying on the street and he wasn't breathing. The other man was studying the prone form impassively from his height.

My legs gave up and I had to lean against the wall for support, fighting to keep the contents of my stomach down. Had I just witnessed a shooting? Worse yet, had I witnessed my boss kill a man?

It took a while before I trusted my legs enough to lean around the corner again. The street was empty. There was no body and no shooter. The latter I could believe—all he had to do was run—but where had the body gone?

Three

I WAS STILL SHAKING WHEN I returned to the shop. Amber took one look at me and hurried across the shop floor to me.

"What's happened?"

I could only stare at her, bewildered. "I think I just saw a man being shot."

She exhaled in shock. "We have to call the police." She reached for the phone on the counter and then halted. "Wait, you *think*?"

"I…" I made a helpless gesture. "There were two men, there was a bang, there was a man lying down, and then there wasn't."

"What do you mean *wasn't*?" she asked sharply.

"I closed my eyes briefly, and when I opened them, both men were gone. There wasn't even a trace of blood on the pavement."

I'd forced myself to go there to look.

"Odd. Did you get a good look at the shooter?"

It was at the tip of my tongue to say it had been my boss, but it was dark and I hadn't seen his face clearly. "No, but it was the man who exited the shop earlier."

She paled. Then she placed a firm hand between my shoulder blades and practically pushed me to the hallway at the back. "I'll handle this. You go to your room and worry about nothing. Breakfast is at seven."

She rushed to the back room to call Luca again, leaving me to lug my bags to the third floor. I didn't want to go to bed—who could after what I'd witnessed?—but I unpacked my bags and forced myself through my evening routine. I had an early morning, and the first day after holidays ahead of me. I needed sleep.

The bed was comfortable and the linen crisp and clean. I tried to stay awake, in case Amber wanted to speak with me, but the long day won. Before I fell asleep, I felt a small weight settle on my feet, even though I could swear the cat hadn't been in the room earlier. The next thing I knew, my alarm was beeping annoyingly and it was six in the morning. No cat anywhere.

I had the bathroom to myself. I had no idea at what time firemen's shifts ended, but I doubted Ashley would be back until later. There could be a fire somewhere that needed extinguishing or something.

I dressed in a sleeveless silk wrap dress Mother had bought for me when we went shopping together in Nice. It was tea green, with a tastefully plunging neckline and flouncing hem that reached to my knees, a perfect combination of summer and work casual. The pink leather sandals were new too, also courtesy of my mother. I wasn't above letting her buy me clothes I couldn't afford. I paid for them by listening to her sermons about my life and my reluctance to marry.

My long hair in a French braid and my make-up light, I headed downstairs for breakfast. Delicious scents reached me already in the stairs, and my mouth was watering by the time I entered the kitchen.

Giselle was at the stove, hopeful Griselda at her feet, and she began to fill a plate the moment she spotted me.

"Good morning, Phoebe. Sit down, I'll bring you breakfast. I trust you slept well?"

"Yes, to my surprise," I admitted as I took a seat at the long table.

"It's not a surprise. I cast a tiny spell. Nothing intrusive, don't worry, just enough to make it easier for you to fall asleep."

I blinked. "So you're a witch too?" I couldn't believe I was asking that.

"Something like that," she said with a smile.

Okay…

A plate so full I couldn't possibly eat everything was placed in front of me. But as if hearing my thoughts, my stomach growled almost painfully. I'd had nothing but a couple of pints the previous day, if you didn't count the airplane breakfast and a sandwich on the train—which you really shouldn't.

"Coffee or tea?"

"Coffee, please."

By the time Giselle returned with the coffee, I'd made good progress with the food. She beamed at me.

"Good. You need flesh around your bones."

I didn't exactly agree. I had enough curves for my liking, and every pound I gained tended to go to my bottom.

"So … did Amber talk about my incident last night?" I finally asked when I was almost finished with my food.

She made a brushing gesture with her hand. "Yes. But don't worry about it. It's all solved now."

"But what was it?"

"Not a shooting," she said with such a firm tone that I didn't dare to ask more. I just thanked her for the delicious breakfast and headed out.

~ ~ ~

THE SHOP WASN'T open at this hour, so I exited through the back door and rounded the building to the street. I gave the shop front a curious look now that I could see it in a better light, and noticed a sign hanging over its door, a black lantern with a name written on it in silver cursive: House of Magic.

Luca had meant it literally, then.

My walk to the Barbican tube station was about half a mile longer, but that was nothing compared to what my commute could have been if I'd had to move to the outer rims of London. My journey to Bond Street Station required one change, but even in the morning rush it took me only forty-five minutes to reach my destination, a quiet pedestrian court off Oxford Street near the station. It was an expensive location next to the tourist routes, but not instantly noticeable by casual passers-by.

Kane's Art and Antiques had two rooms by the street: a shop where we sold antique and curious items tastefully displayed in glass cases, and a larger gallery where we held art and antique exhibitions and auctions. The shop was closed on Sundays and Mondays, and the gallery was currently empty.

The offices upstairs had their separate entrance next to the gallery door. I switched off the alarm and gathered the mail that had accumulated while Kane and I were on our holidays. Sorting it would take the whole morning, but before I began I had the regular morning routines to perform, the most important of which was brewing a pot of tea to Kane's exact liking.

I had everything finished by the time I heard the door downstairs open at nine, signalling my boss's arrival. To my bafflement, my stomach tightened and my hands turned clammy as I waited for him to climb to the upper floor. I'd never had such a reaction to him before. He could be intimidating when angry, but he was always respectful. I had no reason to be frightened of him.

No reason except the shooting I'd witnessed the previous night—the one I wasn't supposed to worry about.

He entered the small lobby where I had my desk and I plastered a smile on my face. Apparently, I didn't quite manage the desired effect of calm competence, because his deep blue eyes sharpened, and a small crease appeared between his straight black brows.

"Good morning, Phoebe. Is something amiss?"

He wore a black three-piece suit like always despite the late August heat. His lean, defined face was impeccably groomed and slightly tanned after spending his holiday in Greece. He looked healthy and relaxed.

Tension in my body eased. I had worked for him for two years. He couldn't have been outside the shop last night. It was utterly silly of me to even imagine it.

But I had to tell him something. "I had a difficult homecoming yesterday. I guess I'm still rattled."

One brow rose slightly, prompting me to explain, so I did. His mouth tightened in displeasure. "I thought you owned the flat?"

"No, but the lease is in my name, so I'm responsible." My parents had rented the flat for me when I went to the university, but I'd paid the rent myself ever since I'd had a proper job.

"Where are you staying now?"

"I already found a wonderful place. You don't have to worry about it." My mobile rang just then, and I grimaced when I saw who was calling. "It's my landlord."

To my surprise, he reached a demanding hand towards me. I gave him the phone and he answered it for me.

"This is Mr Kane, Miss Thorpe's lawyer," he said, the lie smooth, as if my poised and put-together boss did it often.

He listened to the other end, his face darkening with every word my landlord said. The man was a weasel, but I almost felt sorry for him for having to deal with my boss.

"That is unacceptable," he said in response to something the landlord said. "Miss Thorpe will arrange the renovation herself. She will return the keys once it's done."

He ended the call and handed the phone back to me. I stared at him, stunned. "Why did you say that? He would've handled everything, and I wouldn't have had to bother myself with the mess anymore."

"He would've charged you twice the costs and kept the change," he said dryly. He was probably right, but the ache in my stomach returned. I had no idea where to find reliable handymen. But he wasn't done surprising me.

"Don't worry, I'll handle everything." He clapped his hands together. "Now, I believe we have a lot to do if we want to have the new exhibition ready in ten days. So let's get to work. But first: tea."

I loved my job. I'd studied art history in university, and then attended a two-year programme offered by

Hexing the Ex

Sotheby's to learn auctioneering. I would've loved to work for a large auction house like them, but this place suited me infinitely better. At Kane's gallery I could really be part of the process and learn much more than elsewhere.

Most of the time, however, I was a glorified secretary. I kept the books, handled the correspondence, booked the artists, created advertising campaigns, and took care of all the details that Kane found tiresome—and mystifying even.

"Why do we need a webpage?" he'd asked when I first came to work for him and suggested it, as if he was from an earlier era and couldn't quite get the hang of the modern world, though he was only thirty-five. But he had a great nose for art and antiques, so I could overlook his eccentricities.

On top of my regular job, I had to deal with deliveries today too, which on other weekdays were left in care of Mrs Walsh, who supervised the gallery. I'd thought I was clever to time the deliveries to come after we returned from our holidays, but that meant they all arrived today, and there were a lot of them. I was constantly running up and down the stairs, and I was seriously considered taking my laptop to the gallery and working from there.

When the buzzer rang yet again, I summoned all my goodwill as I headed down the stairs to be able to smile at the delivery person. It wasn't their fault that I was fed up with the exercise already.

But when I reached the door, there was no one there. Groaning, aggravated, I leaned out of the door and checked the pedestrian court outside the gallery in case the delivery person was still near, but there were so many people passing by that I couldn't spot anyone.

"You could've waited," I yelled, startling an older gentleman who was studying our window display, and I apologised hastily.

I was about to close the door when I noticed a parcel on the low step outside the door. It was addressed to Kane, not the gallery, but that wasn't unusual. Mollified, I carried it to my desk. It was a fairly large box, but light, so I assumed it contained something fragile. I was proven right when the first thing I saw when I opened it was white Styrofoam pellets.

I dug my hand carefully into the pellets and pulled out the object that met my hand. To my surprise, it turned out to be a fairly sturdy wooden statuette that didn't look like it would easily break. I couldn't immediately discern its age or cultural origin, but it looked vaguely African. It was polished black ebony, about the height of my forearm from elbow to the tip of my middle finger, and roughly the same girth too, and hollow. It seemed to consist of intertwined twirling ropes about the thickness of my index finger, carved lengthwise of the statuette, but when I took a closer look they turned out to be beautifully detailed snakes coiled in some sort of dance of death.

I shuddered in disgust. I didn't like snakes, on top of which there was something vaguely threatening about the statuette, as if the snakes were constantly slithering.

I placed it hastily on my desk and then rummaged in the box for sender details and information about the piece of art. But even after I emptied it of the packaging pellets, all I found was a card with only one sentence written on it by hand. Only, it wasn't in any language I recognised.

Picking up the statuette again, I headed to my boss's office. "This arrived just now," I told him when he lifted his head. He looked annoyed for being interrupted, but he always did. He spotted the statuette and his eyes grew large. I waved the card.

"But there's no sender information or any identification, nothing but this, and I can't even pronounce what's written on it." That didn't stop me from trying.

My boss surged up so fast he sent his chair rolling backwards. "No!" he shouted, but it was too late. I'd already finished my rendition of the text.

There was a weird sensation inside me, as if all my bones and internal organs exploded outwards with a dull puff, but without any pain. My ears whooshed and sight dimmed. I threw a hand in front of me to prevent myself from falling, but the last thing I saw was the floor approaching my face.

Four

I CAME TO ON A SOFA IN Kane's office. I was lying on my back, with a cold compress on my forehead and a pillow under my feet to elevate them. Acute embarrassment filled me as I took in the situation. I made to get up, only to be thwarted by a firm hand on my shoulder pressing me back down.

"Don't try to get up yet. You might faint again." Kane's blue eyes were filled with unprecedented concern as he studied me, but then again, I'd never given him any cause for it before.

A faint blush rose to my cheeks, so I was fairly sure I wouldn't immediately faint. "I ... can't understand why I did so in the first place."

"Have you had lunch today?"

Was that it? "No, I haven't had time."

He shook his head, slightly exasperated. "Why don't I fetch us something and we'll see if that helps."

That was it. I was dying and he didn't want to worry me with the truth.

"I'll fetch it." I pushed up again and was again stopped.

"Do not move."

The stern tone combined with a commanding look was more familiar, so I settled on the sofa again. I absolutely planned to get up the moment he left the room, but I closed my eyes obediently when he told me to.

The next thing I knew, the scent of Indian food filled the room. I opened my eyes to see Kane place a delicious smelling box on the coffee table in front of the sofa. There weren't any Indian restaurants on our street, so he must have ventured farther for it. How long had I slept?

"Eat. You'll feel better."

He waited for me to sit up and take the food container, before sitting at the other end of the sofa with his lunch. We ate in silence that was surprisingly companionable, considering that we didn't often have meals together.

I felt much better once I was finished. "I think I'd best to return to work," I said, getting up. My legs held. "Thank you for looking after me. I'm sorry I fainted like that."

"It was an unusual reaction, to be sure, but you're fine now," he assured me with a smile.

I pulled back, baffled. "Reaction to what?"

He went completely still. "Do you remember what you were doing before you fainted?"

I furrowed my brows as I tried to recall. "Not really." I closed my eyes, racking my brain. "There was a statuette I wanted to show you." I glanced around but couldn't see it. "Where did it go? And was there ... a card?" My mind was blank.

"The statuette is in the safe. It would be best if you didn't touch it again," he said firmly.

I found it odd. We had some valuable items that were kept in the safe, but he hadn't forbidden me from touching any of them. The opposite, in fact, as I was here to learn.

I began to gather the empty food containers to occupy my hands as my mind raced. "I've never seen such an item before. Who was it from? There was no sender."

"That's what I intend to find out." His mouth set in such a determined line that I had no doubt he would succeed.

I busied myself with routines for the rest of the day to avoid thinking about the embarrassing incident. Kane had been gracious about it, but if he thought I was prone to fainting spells, he might find me unfit for working for him and fire me.

I couldn't fathom what had happened. I hadn't fainted in my life. Had I caught a bug on the airplane or something? Should I book a doctor's appointment? Or perhaps I should add iron to my diet for a while…

The day came to an end without more incidents, with the two of us keeping mostly in our own rooms. I was preparing to leave for home when the door buzzer rang once more.

"For God's sake," I groaned. "Aren't they done for the day already?"

I headed down the stairs with angry stomps, not feeling particularly charitable anymore, and pulled the door open with a great force. But it wasn't a delivery person.

"Troy?"

What the heck?

My ex was standing on the step, an expectant smile on his handsome face as if he was sure of a happy welcome. As always, he looked good, the hipster cut of his golden hair carefully careless, his sleek body wrapped in a summer version of business casual in tan, slim-fit trousers and white, form-hugging shirt with its top buttons open and sleeves rolled up. A linen blazer was thrown over one shoulder.

"Hey, love," he greeted me, leaning down for a kiss, but I pulled back.

"What do you mean, *love*? We've broken up."

He spread his arms with a disarming look. "Come now. It was just a spat. Surely you've forgotten that by now?"

I could only stare at him. "You cheated on me."

"It was a mistake." He hung his head, as if contrite. "I've broken up with her."

"And you think I'll take you back?" I felt sick and it had nothing to do with the fainting spell.

"We were perfect together," he pleaded.

Was he for real?

"You belittled me and tried to change me the whole time." To my shame, I'd only figured that out after we broke up.

"I was just trying to push you to your full potential."

The nerve.

"I don't think you even know what that means," I managed to say.

He flashed me a charming smile. "Why don't we have dinner together and you can tell me about it."

"Absolutely not." Did he really think I was so easily led?

"Why not?" He frowned. "Do you have someone else?"

I squeezed my hands into fists to stop myself from throwing the door at his face. "If I do, it's none of your business. We broke up."

Hexing the Ex

His self-confident smile returned. "That would be no, then, which means there's no reason why you couldn't have dinner with me."

"There's the very good reason that I don't want to," I almost shouted.

He pulled back, baffled. "Surely you're not angry anymore?"

I gritted my teeth. "Angry, no. Disillusioned, yes. I know you now and there's nothing you can do to change my opinion of you."

"So that's it. We just go our separate ways?" He sounded hurt, but I didn't believe the emotion.

"We already did." I'd moved on, I realised to my relief. If he had returned before I went on my holiday, I might have been tempted, but I'd had time to think and recover by now.

He frowned, anger pushing through the charming veneer. "You'll never find anyone as good as me."

My temper flared and I wanted to curse and rant at him with the same fury I'd felt back when we first broke up. But I bit my tongue and pulled straight in what I hoped was a dignified manner.

"We are definitely done." But I couldn't leave it at just that. An ancient Chinese curse popped into my head, perfect because it sounded like a blessing. "May you live in interesting times. Goodbye."

I slammed the door in his stunned face and swirled around to march up the steps—only, they weren't where they should. The world tilted in a funny way, and then it was no more.

~ ~ ~

I WOKE UP WITH my boss patting my cheeks. "Phoebe, are you all right?" His blue eyes were brimming with worry.

I looked around blearily and found myself lying at the foot of the stairs. He was kneeled next to me, his leather satchel at his feet as if he had been on his way home when he found me.

"What happened?" I asked, unable to fathom why I was there.

He frowned. "You fainted."

"Again?" I asked indignantly.

"Apparently." His gaze brushed down my body and then he gave me an uncharacteristically awkward look. "You're not … pregnant, are you?"

I pulled back so fast I hit my head on a stair. "Of course not."

He helped me to sit up. "Only, I've heard that women are prone to fainting spells when they are."

You'd think he was Victorian with vocabulary like that.

"Well, I'm not. It's a bit difficult to be when I don't have a boyfriend." I remembered Troy's visit and grimaced. "Although he tried to weasel his way back into my life just now."

"Is that why you're down here?" I nodded, and he gave me a curious look. "What did you do?"

"I didn't take the cheating bastard back, if you're asking. I sent him on his way with a blessing."

He went utterly still. "A blessing?"

"Well, more a curse." I made a vague gesture. "You know, the Chinese one: May you live—"

He cut me off by placing a hand on my mouth, startling me so badly that I stopped at once. "It would be best if you didn't repeat it. Ever. Come, I'll give you a lift home."

He helped me up and my legs held. He fetched my bag, and then I followed him to his car he had in a reserved spot at the other end of the court. It was a sleek red Jaguar I'd only been allowed into twice before.

"Where to?" he asked once we were in.

I fastened the seatbelt. "I don't remember the exact address, but it's on the same street as the old place."

The engine roared to life and soon we were on our way to Clerkenwell through the late afternoon traffic—which meant not very fast.

"Can you tell me exactly what happened with you and your ex?" Kane asked after a while. He didn't usually ask such personal questions, but I had nothing to hide.

"He thought he could simply return to my life after admitting having had another woman the entire time we dated. I got angry and sent him on his way."

He spared me a quick glance from the traffic. "Were you angry when you wished him interesting times?"

My smile was vicious. "Very."

"Hmmm..."

He didn't talk more until we reached the correct street, but I was used to his silences. "Which house is it?" he asked, and I pointed.

"That one, the House of Magic."

He jerked and accidentally kicked the throttle, almost careening the car to the tail of the one in front of us. "What?"

I'd never seen him lose his poise before, and I found it unsettling. "They had a room to let, and I was the first to apply for it."

"Yesterday?"

"Yes. It's a great place and the rent comes with meals."

He drummed the steering wheel with his fingers, and I had a notion that he hadn't actually heard me. "Maybe they can deal with this, then…"

"Deal with what?"

He didn't answer. But instead of just dropping me off, he found a spot by the curb, parked the car, and followed me to the shop. He was a head taller than me and wearing black, so it felt like I was being tailed by a looming shadow.

Giselle was behind the counter and her eyes grew impossibly large when he spotted us. "What's happened?" she sputtered, crossing the shop floor to us.

"I sort of fainted today," I said with a grimace.

"Twice," my boss added unhelpfully.

Giselle's hands shot to her throat. "You poor thing. You have to go rest immediately."

"I'm fine, honestly."

"Then have a bath or lie down until dinner," she said, concerned, guiding me to the hallway at the back.

I turned to my boss. "Thank you for the lift."

He gave a small bow. "Not at all. And please, if you feel poorly tomorrow, take the day off."

That was not going to happen.

With reluctant steps, I headed upstairs. Before the door closed after me, I heard Giselle speak:

"Now, Archibald, what is this really about?"

I was wondering the same myself.

Five

I DIDN'T TAKE A NAP OR BATH, but I did read a book until dinner time instead of organising my drawers like I should have. I arrived in the kitchen and found a strange woman setting the table.

She was in her early thirties, really tall for a woman—she'd be tall for a man—at about six one, statuesque and athletically built; weightlifting or rugby came to mind. Her running leggings and technical T-shirt revealed truly impressive muscles that looked functional instead of just for show. Her head was clean shaven and it suited her extremely well, as it emphasised her striking features: straight nose, generous mouth, high cheekbones and arching black brows. Her eyes were almost black, and a row of earrings decorated one ear.

After a brief halt I put two and two together. "Are you … Ashley?"

I had assumed that a firefighter would be a man, but she could definitely pull off the job.

She startled. "Ashley Grant, yes. Who are you?" Her voice was fairly gruff, but not unfriendly, so I smiled.

"I'm Phoebe Thorpe. I rented the room next to you yesterday."

She smiled widely and rounded the dining table to shake my hand. A really firm shake, but I expected nothing less from someone who looked so strong.

"Welcome to House of Magic."

I nodded. "I thought that was just the name of the shop."

"It's the whole place," she said with a sweeping gesture.

I looked around to see if I could help with the dinner preparations. A stew was bubbling on the stove, and the scent was divine. I asked where the utensils were kept and began to place them next to the plates and glasses Ashley had set.

"Have you lived here long?"

She gave it a thought. "Four years. I was the first lodger Amber and Gis took in when Giselle inherited the house."

"The shop's been here that long?" I asked, amazed. "I've lived in the neighbourhood for almost seven years and I never noticed it until yesterday."

"The shop was here already when Gis's aunt owned the place," she said with an amused smile.

"Huh." I guess I should start paying better attention to my surroundings.

Luca entered the kitchen, only to jump back to the hallway and throw an arm in front of his face dramatically. "Gah, someone close the drapes."

Alarmed, I hurried to the windows and pulled the curtains across.

"Do you have a migraine?" The sun was setting already, and though it wasn't terribly bright at this time of evening, it might still be too much. "Or are you hungover?"

"I'm just extremely sensitive to sunlight," he stated, taking a seat with his back towards the room.

Ashley poked him lightly in the side with her elbow. "Weakling," she chuckled.

He poked her back. "We'll see who's weak come the full moon."

"You'll be cowering in your room like always."

Their bantering ended when Amber and Giselle arrived and dinner began. I learned that they always shut the shop for two hours for this. "We'll open after sunset again for our more … discerning customers."

Apparently, there were more sun-averse people than Luca around.

"Gis told me you fainted today," Amber then noted.

Everyone stopped eating and looked at me. Feigning nonchalance, I shrugged. "No big deal. It's likely just stress."

Giselle's face creased with concern. "What are you stressed about?"

I made a vague gesture with my spoon. "You know, the eviction and moving here. And then my ex-boyfriend showed up today and wanted us to get back together."

"And you don't want that?" Amber asked, scrutinising me with such intensity that I felt acutely uncomfortable.

"Hell no," I huffed. "He had another woman the whole time we dated. Just because he broke up with her is no reason for me to take him back."

Amber nodded. "That would do it."

It sounded like she agreed with me, but I had the oddest notion she meant something else entirely.

"I'll brew you a special tea that'll help you with the stress," Giselle promised.

"Mellow tea?" I teased her, and she laughed.

"No illegal substances in my teas. I grow and mix them all myself."

"Here?" I asked, amazed.

The back yard had barely enough room for unloading a delivery van, and I hadn't seen anything green there.

"We have a cottage outside London where we used to live before I inherited this place. It has a large garden and orchard I make a full use of."

"Which reminds me, we're all going apple picking this Sunday, so leave the date open," Amber said, giving us a stern look. She hadn't told me that the rent included chores as well, but I was perfectly willing to participate.

After dinner, we cleared the kitchen together, and then Amber and Luca returned to the shop. Ashley and I sat down to watch TV, though there was nothing on that either of us was interested in. Griselda showed up too. She hissed at Ashley, who bared her teeth in return like a dog, making the cat jump onto my lap.

"I thought firefighters were all men," I confessed, petting the cat, who licked her paws and pretended she hadn't been frightened by Ashley.

Ashley wasn't offended. "Women have to meet the same physical criteria as men, so that narrows the pool. But, you know, I'm special, so I can easily handle myself."

I decided it would be rude to ask what she meant with special. "I wouldn't be brave enough even if I were strong enough."

"Sometimes bravery is just lack of imagination," she laughed. "I refuse to think about what might happen. I simply follow the procedure and hope it's enough to keep me safe."

"I hope you'll stay safe at your work too," I said, meaning every word.

Hexing the Ex

The lights in the room seemed to flicker and my head spun a little. I closed my eyes, fearing I would faint again, but it passed instantly.

When I opened them, Giselle was by my chair. "What did you do?" she demanded sternly.

I looked at her, baffled. "Nothing. We were just talking about Ashley's job."

"Did you make a wish?"

"No…?"

"She hoped that I wouldn't come to harm at my job," Ashley assured her, but Giselle pinched her eyes closed.

"Oh, that's not good…" She hurried to the kitchen and Ashley and I exchanged bemused looks. She returned a moment later with a large mug of tea.

"Drink this all." And she wouldn't leave my side until I complied. It was good, fragrant tea, unlike anything I'd tasted, so it went down easily. I handed her the empty mug with my compliments, but she just gave me a worried look.

"Just no more wishes, okay?"

"Okay," I said, though I had no idea what she meant.

I don't know what was in her tea, but it didn't take long for my body to start feeling heavy. My eyes wouldn't stay open, and I could barely drag myself to my floor and wash my teeth before I collapsed on the bed. Just before the sleep came, a thought occurred to me:

How did Giselle know my boss by name?

~ ~ ~

I didn't faint again that week. In fact, thanks to Giselle's healthy food, I felt better than I had in ages. She even packed leftovers for me to take to work as lunch, because she didn't believe in sandwiches.

"They have absolutely no nutritional value," she stated when I told her there was a Prêt right across the court from the gallery.

Her care and attention made me feel welcome in my new lodgings, and in a couple of days I felt like I'd always lived there. I liked Luca and Ashley, whom I saw at dinner most evenings, and Amber with her brusque manner was growing on me.

I didn't have time to ponder my health anyway, as pace at work picked up. We were preparing to open an exhibition of contemporary art next week. We didn't often display living artists, and after spending every day with the up-and-coming young painter as he stressed over the perfect placement of each painting, only to change his mind the next day, I was fairly sure I knew why.

Kane left it all for me to handle, and while I was grateful he trusted me enough to do it, I knew it was because he didn't have patience to deal with the artist himself. He didn't bring up my fainting again, but several times I caught him staring at me with an inscrutable look on his face. I asked about the statuette once, if he had found out who had sent it. He said he was working on it and changed the topic.

I could take a hint. But when I had an occasion to check the safe for a different item, I noticed the statuette wasn't there.

Before I even realised, it was Saturday, which I'd decided would be my moving day. Bright and early—i.e., before noon—armed with a stack of boxes I bought from Staples on the way, I entered my old flat for the first time since Sunday.

A welcome sight met my eyes: the ruined carpet had been taken away and two industrial sized dryers were drying the concrete floor. It didn't smell so bad there anymore.

Kane had come through, which shouldn't have surprised me, but did. He was very capable at his job, but he didn't seem entirely practical when it came to everyday life. I was fairly sure he had a housekeeper looking after him at home.

I spent the morning packing my things, with a second trip to Staples for more boxes. Regardless, I was finished by early afternoon, which I found kind of sad. I'd lived there for seven years. Surely I had more to show for it?

Giselle had promised to help me transport the boxes with her van, so I sent her a message and she soon arrived, dressed for the job in a T-shirt, shorts, and trainers.

She took in the ruined foyer and her brows shot up. "Well."

I nodded, slowly. "I know."

Wordlessly, we began to carry the boxes one at a time down three flights of steep stairs. Before long, we were sweating. "If Ashley weren't at work, I would've asked her to help," Giselle panted as we were climbing up for the next round.

"Maybe we could ask Luca?"

She gave me a funny look. "I don't think that's possible at this time."

"Is he working at the shop?"

"No, he's … sleeping."

I found that odd, but maybe the night shift at the shop went till morning and he slept during the day.

Even with just the two of us, we were soon done. I was going through the rooms one last time to check that I hadn't forgotten anything, when Nick walked in, looking exactly like he always did, a bit unkempt and utterly carefree. My heart jumped in delight, much to my surprise, and he smiled brightly too as he pulled me into a hug.

"I'm so glad I ran into you. I was afraid we'd never see each other again."

I'd sort of thought the same. "Did Betty let you move in?"

"Yes? You?"

"I found a room near here." I gave him the address, just in case. "This is my landlady, Giselle."

Nick flashed his most charming smile and kissed her hand. "Lovely to meet you, Giselle."

She blushed slightly and stammered something in return. Apparently married women weren't immune to his charm either, even those married to women.

"Are you here to fetch your things?" I asked, and sighed in silent relief when he shook his head. I wouldn't have had the energy to help him.

"No, I've moved a bag at a time the whole week. I'm just here to check that I've not forgotten anything."

He went through the rooms like I'd done and then returned to the foyer. "I guess this is it, then." He gave me the key. "You'd better handle this."

To my embarrassment, I had tears in my eyes, and I reached for a hug. He squeezed me back. I was amazingly fond of him now that I knew I didn't have to put up with him anymore.

"You take care, Phoebe," he said, pecking a kiss on my cheek.

"You too. I wish you all the best."

Lights flickered and my knees buckled, but Nick was holding me tightly and he didn't notice. But Giselle did.

"What did you say to him?" she asked sharply when Nick had left after goodbyes and promises to keep in touch.

I leaned down to pick up the last box. "I simply wished—"

"No!"

Her stern command made me stop and straighten up. "No what?" I put my hands on my hips in a huff. "What is going on?"

She bit her lower lip. "I … can't tell you."

"Yet you expect me to not accidently do something you don't want me to do?"

"Eh … yes?"

I gave her a hard look. "I think we have to talk."

A T THE SHOP, GISELLE DROVE TO the back yard and we unloaded the van into the small hallway. I eyed the piles of boxes in dismay, the mere thought of having to carry them to the third floor making my muscles ache.

"Let's have lunch first," Giselle declared, likely thinking the same. I tried to follow her to the kitchen to help her with preparations and talk about the issue she had with me, but she stopped me. "Why don't you rest for a while?"

"I'm twenty-six. I don't need to rest all that much during the day." But since I clearly wasn't wanted, I headed back downstairs, just in case the boxes looked more inviting.

They didn't.

I wandered out to the shop instead. Amber had a customer, an older woman who wanted special tea to help with her arthritis, so I went through the place at a leisurely pace by myself.

It certainly was a magic shop, catering to all sorts of witchy needs. The bookshelf had spell and potion books, books about the history of magic and magical artefacts—

I took out the latter to purchase—grimoires, and who knew what besides. The shelf by the counter contained items for practicing magic, like the tarot cards I'd noticed, crystal balls that looked like genuine crystal and not pressed glass—their price tag certainly suggested so—mortars and pestles, and even an honest to God cauldron, though very small.

The last shelf had tea in large tins and all sorts of herbs and roots I couldn't name. They looked like ingredients of a witch's potion.

"No eye of a newt?" I teased Amber when she strolled over to me after her customer left. She grinned and pointed at a bag containing tiny yellow seeds.

"Here."

I leaned closer to read the label. "It's mustard seeds?" I asked, disappointed.

"Yes. All the witches' ingredients in *Macbeth* are plants, despite their more interesting names."

"Thanks for ruining Shakespeare for me," I said dryly, making her chuckle. I gave her the book I was holding. "I'd like to buy this."

Her brows shot up. "You're interested in magical artefacts?"

"I'm interested in antique and curious items, and these fit the bill."

"They certainly do. But don't expect any of these to show up at auctions." She rang my purchase. "You'll get ten percent family discount."

"Thanks," I said, delighted. It was nice to be thought of as family.

She shot me a stern look. "Now, are you going to do something about those boxes that are filling my hallway?"

Luckily, Giselle called me to lunch just then, so I fled the scene with an apologetic wave.

We were having squash soup and freshly baked bread Giselle had made that morning. My mouth watered as I took a seat, placing the book on the table next to my plate.

"No reading at the table," Giselle said with mock sternness, then took another look and picked it up.

"Why did you buy this?"

"Because it looked interesting," I explained for the second time. "I'm an antiques dealer in the making, you know."

"The artefact won't be there."

I'd been about to take a spoonful of her excellent soup, but I put it down. "What artefact?"

She made a vague gesture with her hand, taking a seat too. "The one that caused all this."

I blinked. "Perhaps you should finally explain what all this is."

"I ... should probably talk with Archibald first."

"My boss? And how do you know him anyway?" And well enough to call him by name.

She shrugged. "Everyone in our business knows him."

"Because he's into curious items too?"

I hadn't seen him deal with anything out of the ordinary in my two years working for him. The snake statuette was an exception, and he hadn't put it on display or in our sales catalogue.

"Not exactly, but it's good enough for now." She began to eat, and I resumed my meal too.

"So shall I call my boss or will you?" I then asked to prompt her. She gave me a hopeful look.

"Would you?"

I could understand that she was intimidated by Kane; I occasionally was.

"And what should I tell him?"

Amber walked in just then. "Tell who what?"

"Phoebe made another wish," Giselle told her, and she paled.

"Bugger."

I threw my arms up, spattering soup on the floor with the spoon I was holding. Griselda was instantly on it.

"What is wrong with you people? Why shouldn't I wish well to people I like?"

They both tensed, but nothing happened.

"I guess it only works if it's specific to a person," Amber noted, and Giselle nodded.

"That's something at least."

I banged my hand on the table. "Will you fricking just tell me what is going on already!"

They looked at each other. "I think it's best," Amber said, her face grim.

I couldn't understand them at all. What could possibly be such a secret? And why was it so bad that I wished nice things to people—or not so nice, in case of my ex?

"Do you remember the statuette that was sent to Archibald on Monday?" Amber asked.

"Of course," I said, shuddering. "Who could forget a bouquet of slithering snakes?"

"And the text that came with it?"

I frowned. "No…?" I tried to recall. "There was nothing. No sender and nothing about the artefact."

She pursed her lips. "I really should leave this to Archibald."

"Just tell me."

"Fine." She leaned closer over the table. "The statuette is a powerful ancient curse."

I gave her a slow look. "A curse?"

"That's the simplest way of explaining it," Amber said, ladling soup onto her plate. "The text that came with it activated it, attaching the curse to the person who was holding the statuette when it was read. That would be you."

I had so many questions, most of them starting with "Are you for real?" But I settled with: "What's the curse?"

"Everything you wish for others comes true."

I frowned. "How's that a curse? Shouldn't it be the opposite?" I searched for a suitable word. "A blessing."

"What did you wish for your ex-boyfriend?" Amber asked. She took a spoonful of soup and smiled appreciatively at her wife.

"Interesting times."

She returned her attention to me. "And what sorts of times are interesting?"

I gave it a thought. "The kinds that aren't easy?"

"Exactly," she smiled. "So there's a reason it's a curse."

"But I only wished good things for Nick, my flatmate."

Her eyes sharpened and she put down the spoon again. "All the best?"

"Yes."

"And will he be able to handle a sudden turn in luck?"

My stomach lurched. "No."

Bugger.

My mind was in a whirl. I didn't believe in curses, but Amber and Giselle clearly did. "So, assuming there is a curse—"

"There is," Amber cut me off, and I decided to go with it for now.

"How do I break it?"

Giselle put down her spoon. "I've been doing some research. Only the person who cast the curse can break it. Or you can kill them to break it. Either one works."

I looked at her in dismay. "I'm not killing anyone. Besides, the point is moot. I have no idea who sent the statuette."

"Can't you ask Archibald?"

"I already did. He said he's working on it."

The women exchanged glances. "Maybe we should let him handle it…?" Giselle suggested. I was more than ready to take that option. Anything was better than pretending with them that there was a curse on me.

Angry stomps coming up the stairs interrupted us. Ashley stormed in. She pointed an accusing finger at me and practically growled. It was really impressive. "What the fuck is wrong with you, Phoebe?"

I didn't have to guess what she was talking about. "I just wanted to be nice," I pleaded.

"What did you wish for her?" Amber asked.

"That she wouldn't be hurt at work."

It was a perfectly valid thing to wish for a person in a dangerous job. Giselle seemed to think so too, because she gave Ashley a curious look.

"And how did it backfire?"

Ashley spread her arms, frustrated. "I can't do anything even remotely risky. There was a fire and I was all geared up to go in, but it was as if an invisible barrier was blocking my way. I couldn't get past it."

"You couldn't go where you might get hurt," Giselle nodded, understanding. Ashely marched to a cupboard to take out a plate.

"My boss had to send me home. I'm lucky he's my father so I could tell him the truth, but if this continues, I'll lose my job." She banged the cupboard door closed and began to ladle soup into her plate with such force it sloshed over the rim.

"A curse indeed," Amber noted, rising to fetch a kitchen towel. Ashley took it from her and wiped the table clean with jerky moves. She was really angry.

"You'll have to break it!"

I had tears in my eyes. I hadn't meant to hurt her.

Amber cleared her throat. "I think we'd better set to work."

~ ~ ~

WITH WORK, AMBER MEANT carrying the boxes to my room before anything else was considered. That was for Giselle and me to handle, as she had to return to the shop, but Ashley relented enough to come to our aid. That, or she used the exercise to let off steam, because she was practically running up the stairs with two boxes at the time.

"The curse doesn't seem to affect her now," I muttered to Giselle as we watched in horror how Ashley slipped and almost fell when she took a turn too fast.

"Perhaps it's specific to her work."

A queasy sensation had settled in my stomach ever since Ashley's outburst. As long as we'd been talking about increase—or decrease—of luck, I had been able to think we were dealing in abstracts or, you know, with nonsense. But Ashley's description of her ordeal made it real.

"I hope she won't—"

A hand landed on my mouth, cutting me off. "For goddess's sake: Stop. Making. Wishes!"

I nodded, my eyes large, and Giselle released my mouth. I cleared my throat.

"I don't really believe in curses," I told her as we followed Ashley at a more sedate pace. "Or magic, for that matter."

Her mouth quirked, amused. "But you found here."

"You had a sign in your window," I pointed out. "It didn't really take any detective work on my part."

"But the sign wasn't there for everyone to notice. Only those who suit us could see it."

I shot her a sideways look. "And how exactly would you manage that?"

She smiled. "With magic, of course."

"Which I don't believe in."

"Yet."

I gave it a thought as I stepped aside to let Ashley past on her way down again. "So I'm the one who is cursed? And I just spread it uncontrollably?"

She gestured with her hand, almost dropping the box she was carrying. "It's more like you triggered it and work as a conduit for it to spread."

"But I'm not personally affected by it?" I asked as I helped her to take a hold of her box again. She nodded.

"You can't hex yourself, but it takes a physical toll on you every time."

I pursed my mouth. "The fainting spells?"

"Yes."

"But I've felt great the whole week."

She gave me a conspiratorial smile. "That's because I made a counter spell which prevents the curse from draining you."

"Huh." I thought of my encounter with Nick. "Does that also mean that the effect of the curse is diminished as a result?"

She bit her lip as she thought about it. "I don't know. But I hope so."

I hoped so too, because Nick would not be able to handle sudden fame well.

Then a new thought occurred to me and I paused, only to be almost mowed over by Ashley, who was already running up again. "The statuette wasn't sent for me. It was sent for Kane."

Giselle looked grim. "Yes."

My stomach fell. "So who would want to hurt him?"

"That … is a good question."

"The one that I should ask him?"

"Yes."

Great.

Seven

THE GALLERY WAS OPEN ON Saturdays, with Mrs Walsh handling things with expertise there. She was an elegant woman in her early fifties who always wore designer clothes and genuine jewellery, thanks to her very well-to-do husband. Her hair was in a honey blond bob, and she had a penchant for four-inch heels that still didn't make her even as tall as me. How she could stand in them for days on end was a mystery to me.

She was a calm and composed person, unruffled by even the most demanding customers. As she always said, "If you can handle three boys through puberty to adulthood, you can handle anything."

But today she shot me a harried look as I entered her dominion to check if the boss was there, like he so often was on Saturdays.

"Thank God you're here. You'll have to deal with him, because I don't have energy anymore." She pointed at the gallery, and I didn't have to guess who she meant.

"Monsieur André is back?"

His real name was Andrew Collins, but that wasn't a name that sold art, so he called himself Monsieur André. He was as French as I was, meaning he came from

Hounslow and had grown up listening to the endless noise of Heathrow Airport. He was my age, much too young to be called Monsieur André in my opinion. He smoked cigarettes through a long ivory holder, dressed only in black, and accessorised with huge, garishly coloured scarfs—neon yellow today. He was undoubtedly talented though, so I could overlook his theatrics.

Leaving Giselle, who had accompanied me on my quest, with Mrs Walsh, I braced myself and headed to the gallery. "Monsieur André," I greeted him with the warmest smile I could muster. "Surely you're not working on Saturday?"

His face lit in delight and he leaned over to kiss the air by my cheeks.

"Ah, Mademoiselle Phoebe. I'm so glad you're here. The shop lady doesn't have an artistic bone in her and I need your opinion. I couldn't sleep when I remembered that I'd placed these two paintings side by side. Look how garish they are together! What ever shall I do?"

I took a dutiful look at the paintings in question and could admit that the effect they had side by side was striking. But should I say it aloud? It would only lead to reshuffling of all the paintings, and I had better things to do today.

Then again, it didn't matter what I said. We'd be moving them around every day until the opening. So I nodded.

"You are absolutely right. But is it so bad?"

He pulled back. "Bad? It hurts my eyes."

I nodded, pretending to study the paintings with a critical eye. "I like how it makes me feel inside. Unsettled."

"Really?" He tilted his head and studied the paintings too. "Yes ... I can see it. Feel it. Yes, you are absolutely right. We'll leave it as it is."

I let out a silent sigh. "I'm glad you approve."

He wrapped an arm around my shoulder jovially. "Ah, poor Phoebe. I'm making life dreadfully difficult for you, aren't I?"

"Not at all," I assured him as convincingly as I could. "But I do wish you could make up your mind already."

Oh, bother.

~ ~ ~

I CAME TO ON MY boss's sofa—again. Two people were arguing in low voices behind me, and I strained my ears. Giselle and Kane. Why did she have to involve him?

I must've made a noise, because Giselle leaned over me. "How are you feeling?"

Her brows creased with worry as she helped me to sit up. I held my breath, but I wasn't dizzy anymore.

"I'm fine. I thought you'd made a spell to prevent me from fainting again."

She gave me a pointed look. "And I thought I told you not to make wishes again."

"It's really difficult," I sighed.

Kane handed me a glass of water and I took it gratefully. His face was inscrutable like always. Was he angry with me? Disappointed?

"What did you wish for this time?" he only asked.

I grimaced. "That Monsieur André would make up his mind about the paintings."

A faint smile ghosted his face. "I see."

"Well, I don't," I said, fed up. "I need answers, and they'd better be something else than I'm cursed."

He sat on the coffee table, facing me, and I realised to my surprise that he wasn't wearing a suit, but black trousers and a black V-neck T-shirt. The shirt gave me a glimpse of a really nice, sculpted chest and leanly muscled arms. I'd had no idea he hid those under the layers of clothing he normally wore.

I glance around, my surroundings finally registering. "How did I get here?"

"Mrs Walsh alerted me and I carried you," Kane said as if it was perfectly normal. I felt a blush rise up my chest.

"I ... thank you?"

He patted my knee. "Not at all. Now, are you truly all right?"

"I am," I assured him. "These fainting spells don't seem to have lasting effects."

He pursed his mouth. "Interesting."

"It's anything but," I huffed. "Can you please give me some answers?"

He ran fingers through his hair, aggravated. "Let's just say that I have some powerful enemies and you're unfortunate collateral damage."

I almost snorted in disbelief, only barely managing to keep the noise inside. "Enemies? You? But you're an antiques dealer." The competition could be fierce in our business—thefts weren't unheard of—but surely it didn't go beyond that.

"That's not all I am." I cocked my brows, and he made a vague gesture with his hand. "I'm in a ... position of power ... and there's a power struggle brewing. I thought I'd solved it, but I only managed to make things worse and my enemy sent me the curse."

"That I accidentally triggered?"

"Yes."

Hexing the Ex

I tried to make sense of his words. "That's a pretty strong response. What did you do to muddle things up?" The memory of what I'd witnessed near the magic shop flashed in my mind, and I inhaled sharply. Had it been Kane after all? "You're not in the mafia, are you?"

He grinned, the corners of his eyes crinkling and teeth flashing. He had a nice smile that I saw all too seldom. "No. Not the mafia."

"So what did they hope to achieve with such a strange curse?"

He shook his head, sobering. "I have no idea. But you've already noticed that it's not easy to not make wishes."

I tilted my head in acknowledgement.

Giselle drummed her fingers against her thigh, looking pensive. "Maybe it's not what you'd do with it. Maybe it's about how it would've affected you when you did?"

My boss shot her a sharp look. "What do you mean?"

She faltered briefly in the face of his intensity, but gathered herself admirably. "Every time the curse flows through the conduit, it drains them."

"Hence the fainting," Kane said, nodding.

"But Phoebe is not a powerful conduit, so it doesn't have much to drain, whereas you…" She drifted away. I had no idea why he would be more powerful than I, but he clearly understood, because his face tightened with anger.

"It could've emptied me completely. I would've been powerless. An easy target."

"Or worse," Giselle said, straightening alarmed. "It could've killed you outright."

I didn't like the sound of that.

"Who sent the curse?" I asked.

Kane spread his arms, frustrated. "I have no idea."

"But we have to find out," I pleaded. "Giselle said that only they can break it."

He glanced at Giselle, who nodded. "Or he has to be killed."

His mouth tightened, determined, and I lifted my hands in front of me, as if to ward him off.

"I'm sure we can solve this without excessive violence."

He gave me a level look. "We may not have a choice. We're not necessarily dealing with normal people here."

"Oh, really?" I asked, with as much sarcasm as I could muster. "Because my friends and I send curses to each other all the time."

My sarcasm had no effect. "I mean we're not dealing with humans."

"And what are we dealing with, then?" I asked, not for a moment believing he was serious.

"Black mages or warlocks," he stated, as if that was a perfectly normal thing to say.

"And they're not ... human?"

He shrugged. "Not the way you are."

I let it sink in. "The way I am? Surely you mean we are?" But he just kept staring at me, not answering, so I glanced at Giselle.

"Right?"

She grimaced and placed a hand on mine. "I'm sorry, Phoebe. I know this comes as a shock. But not everyone who looks like a human ... is."

I stared at her, my mouth hanging open. "How can a human not be human?" I gave it a thought. "They're not lizard aliens wearing human faces, are they? Because I saw that TV series and it terrified me."

"Well..." My eyes grew in horror and she grinned. "Not aliens, but the image is apt enough."

I studied the familiar, handsome face of my boss across me and my stomach twisted uncomfortably. "You're saying that if I ripped off the latex mask covering your face, something else would be revealed?"

He rolled his eyes. "No. I'm perfectly human."

"But you just said you're not," I pointed out.

"I'm just ... enhanced."

I glanced at his chest. "I'll say..."

Giselle snickered, and my boss frowned, puzzled, as if he didn't quite catch my meaning.

"There are humans, humans with abilities, and non-humans pretending to be humans who have different abilities," he said.

"And you would be a human with abilities?"

"Yes."

Did I have to drag everything out of him? "And they would be...?"

"Magic in my case."

"And mine," Giselle added.

I turned to her. "So when you say you're a witch, you mean it literally?"

She shook her head. "Yes and no. Any human can become a witch if they learn the craft. It doesn't require inherent magical ability. I'm a witch in addition to what I actually am."

"Which is?"

"A mage."

"Huh." I turned to my boss. "And you're a mage too?"

"Yes."

"And you were both born this way? And can do magic just with a wave of your hand?" I waved mine in the air.

"It still requires studying," Kane pointed out. "And some are better at it than others."

"Some are able to channel more power?" I guessed from what they'd said earlier.

He smiled, delighted. "Yes."

"And there's a power struggle among the mages? And someone tried to hit you at your power."

"Exactly."

I leaned back on the sofa and rubbed my arms. I felt a bit chilly. "And that someone would be a black mage or warlock?" I couldn't believe I was having this conversation with him.

"They are the only mages who deal with curses," he said, nodding. "Though warlocks actually fall into the category of non-humans."

"This is quite a lot to take in."

"And it's not even all of it," Giselle said dryly. I didn't want to think about it, so I pushed it aside and studied them with determination.

"So how do we find this black mage or warlock?"

"We don't find anything. I will handle it," Kane stated firmly. But I wasn't about to let him push me aside. I lifted my chin.

"You've had a week already without results while I keep cursing people I want to be nice to, which wouldn't have happened if you'd told me about the curse in the first place."

"We don't exactly exist in the open," he said, aggravated. "I can't talk about curses to ordinary humans. Besides, I anticipated a faster solution."

"Well, it didn't happen," I said, pushing my advantage. "It's time for a new approach. What have you tried so far?"

He sighed, giving up. "I've tried to track the previous owners of the statuette to find the current one, but the trace runs cold after a nineteenth century French warlock called Laurent Dufort."

I blinked. "That's a very antiques dealer approach of you. Isn't there anything … magical … you could try?"

Giselle perked. "We'll trace for the sender."

"Absolutely not," Kane stated, standing up. "No one touches the statuette."

I lifted a hand. "A non-magical person here. What's a tracing?"

"Anyone who touches an item leaves an energy signature on it," Giselle explained. "There's a ritual for tracing the signatures to their sources."

"That sounds like a practical solution." I tapped my lip with a finger as I gave it a thought. "If we can't touch the statuette, how about the box it came in?"

Giselle and Kane glanced at each other and seemed to communicate silently. "That might work," she said. "But it may have gone through many hands at the delivery service, in which case it would be useless."

"But it wasn't delivered by a service, because it was left on the doorstep. I bet it was dropped by whoever cast the curse." I was warming to my idea. Giselle nodded.

"Do you still have the box?"

I shot up. "Follow me."

I headed to the lobby and across it to a closet that contained everything from cleaning supplies to printer paper. And a lot of empty boxes in a pile in the middle of the floor.

"We've had quite a few deliveries this week and I've just thrown the boxes here," I explained, slightly embarrassed for having to admit my inefficiency. "I sort of thought to use these as moving boxes, but then I didn't have a practical way to transport them from here."

My boss lifted a brow. "I could've helped."

The mere thought made me flush with awkwardness. "Your car isn't exactly … roomy."

He snorted. "That's not my only car."

I didn't have a counter for that.

Ever practical, Giselle began to move the boxes out of the closet. "I'm assuming that the boxes that came earlier this week are at the back."

I joined her and soon enough most of the boxes were in the lobby. "This is the one," I said, picking up one of the last ones and handing it to Giselle. She snatched her hands back and didn't take it.

"It's best that I don't add my energy signature to it. You carry it."

"Where are we taking it?"

"Home. I have everything we need there."

"I'll give you a lift," Kane said. "Let me just pick up my jacket and we can go."

Eight

AMBER WAS AT THE SHOP when we entered. Her eyes grew large when she spotted Kane. Now that I knew he was a magical human, I sort of understood her reaction. Perhaps he was a superstar in the magic community.

I snorted amusedly to myself.

"Archibald! What brings you here?" Amber said, coming to greet him.

"We had to tell everything to Phoebe," he told her, and she shot me a sideways look.

"Everything?"

"Well, a little about mages and curses," he amended.

I made a note of it. I'd have to ask more the moment I had a chance.

"We're doing a tracing," Giselle told her wife, kissing her in passing as we headed to the stairs. "Hopefully we'll be able to find whoever sent the statuette to Archibald."

"Should I wish for a positive outcome?" I asked, partly in jest, but all three practically jumped in horror.

"Absolutely not," my boss said. "There's no predicting how it'll turn out."

"Like with Ashley," I sighed.

"Your ex?" he asked, curious.

"No, Ashley Grant is a lodger here. She's a firefighter and I expressed a desire that she wouldn't come to harm at work, and now the curse prevents her from working at all."

He looked bemused. "That's one way to achieve it."

"Couldn't you do something about it?" I asked hopefully, but he shook his head.

"No, only the caster of the curse has the power to break it."

Bugger.

Giselle led us to the attic, which turned out to be clear, open space with a slanted ceiling and skylights. It was a workroom, with a lacquered wooden floor, a wooden workbench in front of the skylight towards the street, and shelves full of herbs, cauldrons, and other items needed for practicing witchcraft. Everything was neatly in their place and there wasn't dust anywhere.

Giselle went to a shelf and picked up a large map. "This is central London. Since the package was hand delivered, it probably means that the person lives here."

"My challengers likely come from London, so I find it a reasonable assumption," Kane assured her, making her fluster a little for the praise.

She spread the map in the middle of the floor. Then she asked me to place the box on the map.

"It covers half of it," I pointed out. "How are you supposed to pinpoint anything with it?"

"You'll see," she said.

She went to another shelf and took out a large white chalk, the kind that was used for drawing on pavements. She began to draw on the floor with it, holding it sideways so that it made a thick line, first a circle around the map and then swirls and curlicues sprouting from it in an intricate pattern. Complicated though it looked, she didn't hesitate once and was soon done, indicating that she had done it many times before.

Then she fetched four white candles, each the size of a soda can, and placed them on the circle at specific points. I gave her a curious look and she said they were the compass points.

When everything was to her liking, she clapped her hands together. "Right. Phoebe, you stand at the side of the room and don't interfere, because you've already touched the box and it might hone in on you. Archibald, if you could light the candles, counter-clockwise please, when I begin the incantation…"

I moved to the head of the room, where I was farthest away from the circle but could still see everything well. There was no way I would miss this. Griselda emerged from underneath the workbench and I picked her up so that she wouldn't interfere with the tracing either. Or catch fire from the candles once they were lit.

Giselle sat on the floor outside the circle at the southern compass point and crossed her legs, arranging her skirt neatly over her calves. Kane stood at the northern point. He didn't have any matches or a lighter, but before I could point this out, Giselle began to chant.

It was no language I recognised, though the intonation and some syllables reminded me of Romanic languages, with hints of Latin in the mix. Her eyes closed, her voice rose and lowered, the ebb and flow natural like her breathing. And every time there was a brief lull as she inhaled, a candle lit up. Kane didn't even move, yet he managed to light the candles, starting from the northern point and working counter clockwise, one by one, like Giselle had asked.

I could only stare in awe—and slightly scared. I'd worked for Kane for two years, yet I'd never suspected he could do something like this.

As the last candle lit, a whoosh went through the room. Not like a wind, more a silent implosion that sucked energy into the chalk circle. The box on the map rose in the air, held up by an invisible force. It twirled, and finally settled so that one corner was pointing at the map. It moved up and down over the map, as if searching. It drew towards our location, only to be pushed away by something Giselle said. And then, as if pulled by a magnet, it landed on a spot and stayed there, unmoving despite the gravity-defying position."

Giselle exhaled. "There."

She and Kane leaned closer to take a look, careful not to disturb the chalk circle. Griselda expressed her wish to be put down by pressing her nails into my arm, so I released her and she went to look at the map too. To my amazement, the circle prevented her from entering.

"Holland Park," Kane noted. Then he frowned. "I don't know any warlocks living there."

"Or mages either," Giselle added, and they both nodded. Then my boss smiled, pleased.

"Thank you, Giselle. I'll take it from here."

I perked instantly. "Not without me you aren't."

Kane pivoted to me. "Surely you're not proposing that you'll come with me?" he asked, almost comically stunned, as if it had never even occurred to him that I might want to have a say in solving this.

I lifted my chin up. "I want to be there the moment you find them so I can persuade them to break the curse."

He glared at me. "But it could be dangerous."

"Hardly," I huffed. "If this person was violent, they wouldn't have resorted to such a roundabout method of harming you."

"Be that as may, they still have powers you can't imagine and cannot possibly protect against," he explained, exasperated, but I was undeterred.

"And exactly how much worse do you think my situation can get?"

He opened and closed his mouth a few times, as if unsure how to deal with me. I'd never opposed him quite this firmly before. Then again, I hadn't had a reason to.

Giselle stepped in: "Why don't we all go? That way you'll have backup if needed."

"Excellent idea," I said, before Kane had a chance to oppose her suggestion. "And maybe we can ask Ashley too?"

"Now look," he started, appalled. "Backup is all well and good, but I can't go into a dangerous situation with three women."

I placed my hands on my hips in a huff. "Why not? Is it not cool enough?"

"No, but that's one more person I might have to protect," he said.

Giselle snorted. "I can assure you, Ashley can protect herself. And us too, for that matter."

Kane pinched the bridge of his nose, looking pained. "Fine. It's not as if I can stop you."

Giselle and I shared triumphant smiles and then headed down one floor, where she went to knock on Ashley's door. While she was handling that, I wandered to my room to change into something more suitable for confronting a warlock than a flimsy summer dress.

"Is this your cat?"

I swirled around to see that my boss had followed me in. He was holding Griselda, who was purring like an excitable engine.

"No, Griselda belongs to the house."

Scratching the cat between her ears in an absentminded fashion, he looked around and spotted the boxes that filled one side of the room, waiting to be unpacked. He gave me a puzzled glance.

"I thought you moved already on Monday?"

He probably thought I was completely incapable of handling practical matters.

"I fetched my belongings today," I hastily assured him. "Which reminds me, thank you for arranging the repairs. They were well underway."

He sketched a small bow. "Happy to help. The owner of the firm owes me a favour, so I'm sure he'll do a good job."

"I'm sure my former landlord will find something to complain about it anyway," I said dryly, making him sneer.

"He can try."

The look on his face sort of made me wish that the landlord would.

Should I express it aloud?

I checked myself. Less than a week with the curse—one day knowing that it existed—and I was already eager to abuse it.

When Kane just stood there, looking around with interest, I cleared my throat. "I need to change."

He lifted his brows, baffled. Then he understood. "Oh, sorry." He retreated hastily to the hallway, taking Griselda with him.

Hexing the Ex

I made a quick change into jeans and a T-shirt, both slim-fit and black. Trainers for walking silently, in case we had to sneak around; hair into a braid, and phone in the back pocket for extra safety, and I was ready to go.

The rest of our little party had retreated to the kitchen, where Giselle was making dinner. "We're not going anywhere without eating first," she stated.

I was itching to go; the faster we found the person who sent the curse, the quicker I would be free of it, but I already knew better than try to prevent her from feeding people. Kane seemed to know this too, because he was sitting at the head of the table, looking almost like he was happy to be there.

I'd occasionally wondered about his family life, but had never been bold enough to ask, and Mrs Walsh, who had worked for him longer, hadn't been much of a help either. He never spoke of a spouse or children, so I was fairly sure he was single. But for the first time I came to wonder whether he had friends. Perhaps his life as a mage required such secrecy that he couldn't befriend ordinary people, and if Amber and Giselle were any indication, other mages were in awe of him.

As was Ashley, I noticed to my bemusement. Or maybe she was frightened of him, which didn't make any sense. She was taller than him and clearly more muscled; she could take him in a fight. Yet she was sitting at the other end of the long dining table stiff as a plank, her eyes fixed on him as if she feared he would attack her and she needed to be ready.

I wanted to ask if she was a mage too, but the others might be upset with me for bringing it up if she wasn't. Then again, she was attending a search party for a warlock, so perhaps she was in the know…

Before I could ask, Luca walked in and, like every evening, requested for the drapes to be drawn, which I went to do for him. When I returned, he was sitting next to my boss, talking excitedly about something, only to fall silent when he noticed I had come close enough to hear him.

I ignored his secretive behaviour. If he was a mage too, he'd done it all his life. "Are you coming with us to locate the person who sent the curse to Kane?" I asked.

He perked. "You've found him? Absolutely I will, provided that we wait for the sun to set."

"What is it with you and the sun anyway?" I asked, curious.

Before he could answer, my boss spoke: "Remember what I told you about enhanced humans?" I nodded. "Some enhanced people are more nocturnal."

I blinked, trying to decipher his meaning. "What, you mean like … vampires?"

Nine

"UMMM … KIND OF EXACTLY?" Luca said, and I snorted.

"Like they're real. What, you sleep in coffins and drink blood? Do you change into a bat too?" I laughed aloud at the thought.

"No bats, and coffins are optional," he said with a smirk. "But blood…" He licked his lips in a very provocative way. I shuddered.

"Eww. I'll pass."

"You don't know what you're missing," he sing-songed.

Kane interrupted our bantering: "Perhaps we should concentrate on the issue at hand. We need to make a plan. Do some reconnaissance."

I took out my phone. "Maybe I can pull the satellite image on my phone. What's the address?"

Giselle told me, and my boss leaned over my shoulder as I opened the map. "Street view looks perfectly ordinary, but it's a two-year-old photo." I switched to satellite. "There doesn't seem to be anything odd with the house or the back garden either."

He took the phone from me and studied the image closely. "Is there any way to have real time data?"

"Not with my means."

He pursed his lips, disappointed. "So we can't tell if there are traps or guards at the place."

I gave him a baffled look. "Why would there be guards?"

"Non-humans occasionally employ them."

My stomach tightened. "What kind of guards could we be dealing with?"

For the first time I wondered if it was so smart of me to tag along on this mission after all.

He shrugged. "Anything, really. Hellhounds most likely, or werewolves."

Ashley growled, startling me. "Weres wouldn't guard warlocks."

"They might not have a choice," Kane said with a pointed look. "And it could be a mage just as well."

Ashley pushed herself up, clearly gearing for a fight, so I lifted my hands, halting her.

"Whoa, now you want me to believe in werewolves too? In addition to vampires—which I still don't," I added, glaring at Luca, who just grinned.

"Enhanced humans come in many forms," my boss said, as if that made sense. "The most important thing is to know how to counter them, should there be any."

"Most of them react to … enhanced … humans," Luca said, waggling his brows at the word. "But might let an ordinary human pass."

Kane pulled straight. "Absolutely not. It's too dangerous."

I was a little slow on the uptake, but then I nodded. Apparently I was the only ordinary human here. "I can do it. I'll walk to their door, ring the doorbell, and ask the person who answers to break the curse."

"You will not risk yourself," Kane declared.

"Then how do you propose we do it? You can't just walk to the door by yourself. They're after you and might attack."

"I can handle that," he said, with a hint of arrogance in his sneer.

"How about we all stand at their door so they'll know there are witnesses," Giselle suggested in a placating tone. "That way, they might be more reluctant to act with violence."

She began to lift pots to the table, and I hurried to set the plates. In short order, we settled down to eat. Amber arrived for dinner too, and we didn't talk about the plan anymore.

I didn't really know how to take it all. They seemed so earnest in their belief that we were dealing with non-human entities, or at least individuals capable of great evil.

Then again, if the curse was real, the caster of the curse had to be real too.

"You're not going to kill the person on sight, are you?" I had to ask my boss. He put down his utensils and wiped his mouth with a napkin.

"No. I don't kill people as a rule. Besides, it could be they're working for someone else, in which case I need to ask questions."

That was something at least.

Eventually, the sun set and we filed into two cars, Kane's Jag and Ashley's large Range Rover, with Luca and me riding in the Jag. Luca made me sit in the back seat, which wasn't entirely comfortable. Luckily, the drive to the west side of Hyde Park to the affluent neighbourhood of Holland Park was fairly fast at that time of evening, and we reached our destination before my legs died completely. We left the cars a street over and proceeded to the house on foot.

This corner of Holland Park was full of mid-nineteenth century redbrick houses and terraces, with white trimmings and small, carefully-maintained front gardens. The house we wanted stood alone at the end of its street, the back garden overlooking the park that gave the area its name.

"Whoever this person is, they have money," I noted.

"Most non-humans are wealthy, as they've had centuries to accumulate it," Kane said.

I gave him a curious glance. "Do enhanced humans live longer too?"

"Some do."

I studied him as he walked ahead of me to the house. Was he older than he seemed? It would explain his old-fashioned manners and his inability to comprehend some modern ideas. I found the thought so unsettling that I pushed it out of my mind.

"Do you want to know how old I am?" Luca murmured to my ear.

"Five?"

"Ouch."

The truth was I didn't want to think about his age, like I didn't want to think about the possibility that he might be a vampire—or even the possibility that vampires were real.

Or werewolves, for that matter. But when Ashley suggested that she do a perimeter search because her sense of smell was the best and everyone agreed with her, I had to at least entertain the possibility.

Hexing the Ex

Perhaps she was simply enhanced in the olfactory department.

She soon returned and informed us that there were no guards, humans, enhanced or non-humans alike. As we hadn't been able to come up with a better plan than what Giselle had suggested, we climbed the long steps from the pavement to the front door as a group—a tight fit as there was flower bushes on one side and a drop to the driveway outside the garage under the house on the other.

"I'll stand at the front," Kane said. "The rest of you, block the steps, in case he tries to run."

We did as we were told. Then he rang the doorbell and we waited in tense silence for someone to answer. "What if he's not home?" I asked in a low voice, only then coming to think of that option. Luca snickered, but fell quiet when the sound of a lock being turned came through the door. The door opened and my jaw dropped.

"Troy? What the hell?"

~ ~~

MY EX LOOKED AS flabbergast as I felt. "Phoebe? What are you doing here?"

He wore a pair of seldom-seen-on-him jeans, and a T-shirt that became his slim body well. His golden hair was a bit mussed and there was a five o'clock shadow on his usually cleanly-shaven chin. He gave the people with me a curious look. "And with an entourage too."

I could barely speak, I was so stunned. "Me? Since when do you live here?"

He smiled, slowly. "Oh, I'm not living here. Yet."

"Then who does live here?"

He propped a shoulder against the doorjamb. "Wouldn't you like to know…"

"I would like to know," Kane said firmly, claiming his attention. Troy frowned.

"You're Phoebe's boss, aren't you? Why are you here?"

Kane gave Troy a level look. "To find out who lives here."

"My girlfriend lives here."

"Girlfriend?" I exclaimed, unable to keep it in. "That was fast. Or did you have more than one woman in reserve when we were dating?"

He smirked. "She's new. I have you to thank for her, actually."

My stomach tightened. Did he know about the curse? "Oh?"

"I met her at the café near the gallery after I'd been to see you. She's everything I've ever dreamed of in a woman, and we hit it off immediately. I've barely been home since." He leered, as if I couldn't catch his meaning otherwise.

"I'm glad I could help," I said with as much sarcasm as I was able to muster. Wasn't the curse supposed to make his life worse, not better?

He leaned closer. "Turned out dumping you was the best decision I've ever made."

I inhaled, outraged. "Dumping me? I dumped you, you cheating rat bastard weasel!"

The nerve of him.

He lifted hands in front of him in a placating manner. "Come now, there's no need to get excited. We both know how it went."

Was he for real? "You were begging for me to take you back less than a week ago and now you're pretending it didn't happen? Are you addle-brained?"

He gave me a slow once-over. "Right, like I would be begging you."

I surged forward, only to be stopped by Luca's surprisingly unyielding arm around me. "Why don't we step back and let Kane handle things?"

"Let me go!" I struggled against his hold. "I'll wring his neck."

"I'll wring it for you," he promised magnanimously. "Just calm down."

"Calm down? I wish he—"

His hand covered my mouth. "No wishing, remember?"

"Not even for his dick to shrink?" I asked through his fingers.

He shrugged. "I guess that would be okay…"

"No wishes," my boss said sternly, and then turned to address Troy. "I'd like to meet your girlfriend."

Troy pushed his hands into the pockets of his jeans. "Why?"

Kane sneered. "Maybe I want to give her a choice…"

That was the most provocative thing I'd ever heard him say. It stunned me so thoroughly that I stopped struggling against Luca's hold. Troy didn't quite know how to take it either.

"Right … let me check." He made to close the door, but Kane stoppered it with his hand.

"Why don't we all come in and have a chat."

"All of you?"

"I'll stay here and keep watch," Ashley said, and then pointed at Luca. "You go check the back garden."

Luca released me—not that he'd been holding me tightly anymore—and jumped lightly down to the driveway, as if the drop wasn't at least three metres. I headed in with Kane and Giselle.

An elegant hallway opened from the door, with stairs up on the right and the door to the sitting room on the left, with two more doors at the back. Troy ushered us into the sitting room, but didn't follow us.

"I'll go fetch Amelia."

He disappeared, leaving us to stand in the middle of the room feeling awkward. I was, at least. Kane looked perfectly at ease. He glanced around, chose a wingback chair by the fireplace, turned it a little so that it faced the door, and took a seat, opening the button of his jacket. He stretched his long legs before him and leaned an elbow on the armrest, to all appearances calmly waiting for whoever would show up.

I couldn't settle down. I walked around the room, touching and turning the small items, automatically evaluating them. There were some fine etchings, but otherwise nothing truly remarkable or expensive. Either they'd spent all their money purchasing the house—entirely plausible—or they didn't care for finer things. Philistines.

I did not want to meet the woman Troy thought was the embodiment of his dreams. I knew it hadn't been me; otherwise he wouldn't have had another woman the whole time we dated. But it still aggravated me to know that he had moved on when I had barely recovered from our breakup.

A gentle hand landed on mine that was squeezing an imitation Meissen porcelain figurine. "Easy," Giselle said. "He's hardly worth the expense of that thing if you break it."

"It's not genuine," I said, but I put the shepherdess down.

She grinned. "You can't be too upset if you managed to spot that."

"Phoebe has a good eye," my boss said from his chair.

I blushed faintly. "Thank you." Then I sighed. "What shall we do now? What if Troy's new girlfriend is the one who sent the statuette?"

"That's what I want to ask her," he said calmly.

The door opened just then and Troy entered with one of the most stunning women I'd ever seen in real life. She was tall and slim, with natural curves that were on perfect display in the form-hugging yoga outfit she wore. Her black hair reached to her waist in sexy waves that looked genuine and not like extensions, and her makeup emphasised both her large almond eyes and her full lips.

I felt frumpy in my all-black getup that I'd chosen for sneaking around in, not for impressing my ex. Not that I wanted to impress him, but I didn't want the difference between me and his new girlfriend to be quite this pronounced either.

She paused inside the door, her pose perfect like a ballet dancer's, and honed instantly in on Kane. It had been his purpose, but the interested flash in her eyes irritated me. She'd already taken one man from me. She should keep her hands off him.

I startled. Neither of the men was mine. There was no reason to feel so proprietary. But if she tried to hurt Kane, she would feel my wrath.

Maybe I should make a wish…

Kane gestured towards the other wingback chair, as if this were his house. "Please, take a seat, Miss…?"

"Spencer, Amelia Spencer," she said, sitting down gracefully. Even her voice was sexy, dark and purring. I hated her.

"Miss Spencer, I'm Archibald Kane." He paused, but her face showed no reaction. Either she was very good at keeping her thoughts inside, or she didn't recognise his name. "Is this your house?"

"It belongs to my father," she said, shaking her head so that the long hair flounced lightly. Kane cocked a brow.

"Would I be acquainted with him?"

She shrugged. "I wouldn't know. Are you in the wine import business?"

"Antiques."

"Ah." Her reaction was so bland that she probably hadn't delivered the packet, despite meeting Troy near the gallery; otherwise, she would've made the connection. Pity. I was perfectly willing to cast her as the villain of the piece.

"And where is Mr Spencer tonight?" Kane continued.

Why didn't he ask about the statuette?

"At his lodge meeting."

This made Kane perk a little. "Freemasons?"

She made a vague gesture with her hand. "It's new, and I've never asked, but I don't think so. Now what is this all about?" She glanced at Giselle and me and dismissed us as inconsequential. "Troy said you wanted to meet me."

Kane nodded. "And now I have." He reached into the inner pocket of his blazer and fished out a calling card. "Could you give this to your father and ask him to contact me?"

Her beautifully arching brows furrowed slightly as she accepted the card. "Of course."

"Good." In a fluid move, Kane rose and buttoned his jacket. Then he offered her a small bow. "Thank you for your time."

He headed out of the room, and Giselle and I hurried after him, his sudden exit taking us by surprise.

Troy followed us. "What was this all about, Phoebe?"

I glanced at him over my shoulder. "Grownup business. Don't worry your pretty little head with it." Utterly pleased with my answer, I walked calmly back to the street.

Ten

"Well?" Ashley demanded the moment she and Luca joined us. "Is the curse lifted?"

She was the one to whom it mattered the most.

"I'm afraid not," Kane told her as we headed to the cars. "Miss Spencer didn't register in any ways magical, and the actual head of the household wasn't home. I didn't recognise his name though, so he's not a mage. He could be a warlock, so I have to keep an eye on this place."

"I'll do it," Ashley said. "It's not like I can return to work until this is solved. Luca will take the night shifts."

"Hey!" Luca protested, but she shot him a stern look.

"It's high time you do something useful with your life."

"I help at the shop all the time."

She just snorted in return.

"I would be grateful if you could do that for me," Kane said. "At least for a couple of days. Maybe this lodge of his is the key to all this, so if you could find out with whom he meets and where, that would be good. But please, don't try to approach him."

Ashley patted Luca on the shoulder. "I'll come back for you well before sunrise," she promised. Grumbling, he returned the way we'd come.

I slumped, dissatisfied, on the front seat during the drive back to the magic shop. Even the Jag couldn't cheer me up. "All that build-up and nothing to show for it," I sighed.

Kane spared a glance at me from the traffic. "We have a name of the potential mage or warlock, and we learned that your hex has taken effect."

I crossed my arms over my chest petulantly. "It was supposed to make his life miserable, not land him the hottest woman on the planet."

He laughed. "You wished him interesting times. Trying to hold on to a woman like that would qualify. And if she gets him involved in mage business, even unknowingly, things might get really hairy soon."

I could only hope.

He pulled over outside the shop, but didn't switch off the engine. "Are you home tomorrow in case I need you?" he asked.

My heart skipped a beat. He'd never indicated that my input mattered to him. Then I realised he meant the entire household and I deflated a little.

"I'm afraid not. We're headed to Amber's and Giselle's farm to pick apples."

His eyes lit up. "That sounds like fun. Maybe I can join you?"

I couldn't keep the stunned look off of my face, and he grinned.

"I'm not completely useless, you know. Besides, Ashley won't be able to participate because of me, so it's the least I can do."

"In that case, I'm sure Amber and Giselle would love to have you with us."

Turned out, I was wrong.

"You did what?" Amber shrieked when I told her about it as I cut through the shop. "You can't ask someone like him to take part in such a task."

"I didn't ask him," I said, miffed. "He volunteered."

"Then you should've discouraged him."

I kind of thought she was right, but I only shrugged. "It'll do him good. I think he's a bit lonely. And Ashley won't be there, and we could use the help."

"And who's going to help me at the shop tonight when you've left Luca to watch over the mage's house?"

Apparently, Giselle had had a chance to brief her already. I was exhausted and my body ached for the unaccustomed physical labour I'd done that day, but I stifled a yawn.

"Maybe I can help?"

"Well, you'd better, because there's no one else around."

I should've known that meant climbing down to the basement and carrying up boxes of merchandise for her. My body protested every step.

It was the first time I'd ventured into the cellar. I don't know what I expected, but a nice airy space with clean floors and rows of metal storage shelves on two sides of a centre aisle wasn't it. Everything was neatly organised and labelled, and I had no trouble locating the boxes Amber needed.

At the other end of the aisle was an open door. Unable to resist the temptation, I peeked in. It turned out to be Lucas's studio flat. It was about the size of Ashley's and my rooms combined, with an en suite bathroom, a kitchenette, and a walk-in closet. It was a perfectly normal bachelor pad, with a large unmade bed, a computer desk with three monitors in a row, a huge TV mounted on the wall, and discarded clothes everywhere. The colour-scheme followed that of the upstairs, with grey walls, white trimmings, and a grey wall-to-wall carpet. The only difference was that the strip windows near the ceiling that gave towards the street were boarded shut.

I still didn't believe Luca was a vampire, but if he was, he was a great aesthetic disappointment. Where were the red walls, velvet drapes, and satin sheets? Or coffins, gilded candelabras, and chandeliers?

The computer gave a beep, and one of the monitors flashed and came on. I simply had to know what was displayed on it, so I tiptoed closer and leaned in.

"Boo!"

Shrieking, I jumped back and almost fell on my bottom when my foot caught in something lying on the floor. Luca's laughing face watched me from the monitor.

"Snooping, are we? You could've just asked and I would've shown you around. I'm a nice and helpful chap, you know."

My heart thumping for the fright and my face red for the embarrassment, I gathered myself. "You're a great disappointment for a vampire. That's what you are."

I swirled around and exited the room with as much dignity as I could muster. Luca's laughter followed me out.

~ ~ ~

DESPITE THE LATE NIGHT, I was up bright and early the next morning. Well, before nine anyway. It was Sunday, after all.

Hexing the Ex

The day promised to be as fine as any we'd enjoyed the whole week, so I dressed for a day of apple picking in khaki capris and a cute T-shirt. I also applied a generous layer of sunscreen. Just because I'd tanned lightly in France didn't mean my sun-averse skin wouldn't burn instantly. My head and face were covered with a large-brimmed straw hat.

Who needed Mediterranean holidays when London offered weather this beautiful?

I did. I needed them.

Despite the early hour—for a Sunday—Kane was already seated at the kitchen table when I showed up for breakfast, emptying his plate with a gentlemanly relish. The sight of him startled me, either because I'd forgotten that he was going to attend—not likely—or because I'd thought he would change his mind.

He was dressed in tan trousers, leather boots, a collarless linen shirt with the top buttons open and sleeves rolled up to the elbows, and a green tweed vest as if he were a gamekeeper at a stately home—or the landlord. I wasn't entirely surprised by the getup, but seeing him in anything but black was definitely mind-boggling.

He smiled when he spotted me. "Good morning, Phoebe. It's a fine day for apple picking."

"It is," I said feebly, taking a seat next to Amber, unable to process the sight of him. I wasn't sure what word would describe him best, but "wow" came pretty close. I wasn't used to thinking of my boss in terms of wow-ness and I found it utterly disturbing.

"We're taking Ashley's car," Amber told me, as Giselle put a plate in front of me. "It's large enough for us all."

I forced my attention back to the matter at hand. "Did Luca get home safely?" I asked, although after his prank, I wasn't entirely sure I cared.

Fine, I cared.

She nodded. "He had an uneventful night. Mr Spencer returned before midnight and no one else came or went the rest of the night."

That would include Troy. The thought soured my mood.

"And has Mr Spencer contacted you yet?" I asked my boss, who shook his head, making his permanently windblown hair sway.

"I don't expect him to call before Monday, if then."

"Maybe we should pay him another surprise visit?" I suggested.

"I'm afraid the element of surprise is gone."

He was probably right. Even if Mr Spencer was a mere errand boy who had delivered the packet, he would surely rush to inform his master that we were on to them and they would devise a plan to stop us. Our only hope was that Ashley could follow him there.

After breakfast, we piled into Ashley's car and Amber drove us to Esher, a small commuter town twenty miles southwest of London full of quaint houses and countryside. The drive went pleasantly, with Kane and Amber exchanging stories of difficult or odd customers. If you thought the magic shop had the most bizarre ones, you'd be wrong.

I asked Kane what I'd been itching to know: "Do you ever deal with occult items like the curse statuette?" Maybe those things passed through our shop all the time and I hadn't noticed.

He was sitting at the front next to Amber and he turned to look at me over the backrest of his seat. "No. Such items should never be sold. But I've retrieved a few for the Council of Mages for safekeeping."

"There's a council?" I asked, bemused. "How … mundane of you."

I imagined grey-bearded men in black robes sitting on benches of a chapterhouse, arguing with whoever held the centre stage.

He smiled. "Mages are too powerful to be left unregulated."

"They condone to being regulated?"

He shrugged. "Most of the time."

I leaned forward. "And if they don't?"

"Curse statuettes happen," he stated.

I pondered his words, trying to reconcile my imaginations with the present company. Amber and Giselle were mages and didn't exactly fit my image. Kane, however…

"Are you their leader?" I couldn't believe I hadn't come to think of it sooner.

He nodded. "Yes. Though if my opponent gets their way, not much longer."

"So who's your opponent?"

He frowned. "I don't know."

"How does that work, then?" I asked, baffled, and his mouth quirked.

"Traditionally, the way the competition announces their candidacy is to challenge the current leader in a battle of magic that tests both their skills as mages. The stronger mage wins. But they can start the challenge before they make the announcement."

"Sort of blindsiding the current leader?"

He smiled, pleased that I'd figured it out. "Exactly. There has been one unusual challenge already, so I know I have competition."

"And the curse was their next move?" I guessed. "Or was it a challenge from a different mage?"

He spread his arms. "Either way, it's not an acceptable salvo. A curse can't be broken by the person cursed, so it doesn't measure their skills as a mage."

I pursed my lips. "So instead of challenging you, they've basically tried to move you out of the way."

He looked grim. "Yes."

"That's not nice." I felt annoyed for him.

Giselle tapped her lips. "It's not a large pool of names that would try for the leadership. I can only think of three who are strong enough to challenge you. There's Cynthia Griffin, of course, but she's a bureaucrat and would never do anything underhanded." Amber and Kane nodded. "Then there's Seth Duncan. He's weasely, but an outright attack isn't really his style. And Jack Palmer is definitely strong and ambitious, but he's not thirty yet."

"I'd only just turned thirty when I was selected," Kane reminded him. "Strength is the only thing that matters here."

"But if they have to resort to a curse, it could be this person is not, in fact, strong enough to challenge you," Amber pointed out, as she headed out of the motorway.

"But removing me won't make them a leader, because the remaining candidates will still have to face the challenge, except this time with each other," Kane said.

"Unless the goal is to wipe out the entire competition one by one until they're the strongest one remaining," I suggested.

Hexing the Ex

He turned to me. "That would be disturbing. And sounds more like an attack by a warlock or a black mage."

"Are black mages allowed to challenge for leadership?" I asked.

"No. They're not part of the council. That's what makes them black," he explained.

"I thought it referred to how they use their magic for evil or something."

He gave me a slow smile. "And that's why they're not allowed into the council."

"It's not solely that they use their magic for evil," Giselle said. "The way they practice their magic isn't acceptable either, no matter the cause. Curses are the least of it. There are forbidden spells and ingredients, and live animal sacrifices."

"And human," Amber added, negotiating the narrow streets of the town. "But once they cross that line, they become warlocks and shed all humanity."

I shuddered.

"So we should hope that the person who sent the curse isn't one of those, then…"

"Definitely." Kane rubbed his chin. "It's not merely for me that I need to solve this—or for you and your friends who have already been cursed. If such a person gets their hands in the council, they will put humans at risk too."

Eleven

AMBER AND GISELLE'S COUNTRY HOME was a delightful grey stone cottage from the eighteenth century, with a thatched roof, white-framed windows that were all different sizes, and ivy crawling on the walls. A low fence made of natural stone separated it from the street, and tall hedges from all other sides. It had once stood there alone, but now rows of fairly large houses with landscaped gardens surrounded it, built to accommodate the hordes of City bankers fleeing London.

The small front garden was full of late-blooming roses, their cloying scent making me dizzy. A slated path led from a wooden gate to the front door.

"Don't you have cameras monitoring the place?" I asked, worried, when I couldn't detect any. "A house like this all alone for long stretches of time practically calls for burglars."

A corner of Amber's mouth lifted up. "We're mages, remember? Warding the house against intruders is the best use for our skills."

Right.

Inside, the place was even more perfect. It had been renovated at some point in its recent past, but with good taste that respected the quirks of its architecture and spirit. The walls were whitewashed, doorways were low, and dark support beams cut across the rooms. Dozens of bunches of drying herbs and flowers were hanging from the beams, forcing Kane to bend his head every time he walked under them, and making the interior smell even more strongly than the exterior.

I sneezed, and Giselle shot me a concerned look. "The scent can be a bit overwhelming if you're not used to it. Let's head to the garden."

It was accessed through the kitchen that was clearly the heart of the house and the place where the magic—literally and figuratively—happened. Copper pots and pans that looked like they'd come with the house were hanging over the wood burning cooking stove; mortars and pestles in different sizes and materials covered the shelves; and an iron cauldron rested on the stove. The walls were whitewashed and the tops of the counters were thick oak and well-used.

A door opened to a patio that was paved with red tiles. A white cast-iron seating group was placed under the kitchen window and a pergola protected it from winds. A couple of low steps led to the garden proper. And what a garden it was.

I'd only ever seen such places on TV or in glossy magazines. The vast space was filled from side to side with flower benches in various heights, with barely enough room between them for the winding paths that were paved with the same red tiles and lined with red bricks. There were flowers still in bloom everywhere. I recognised only a fraction of them.

"The herb garden is there at the right," Giselle explained to me as she led us down one path to the back of the garden. "But most of it has been harvested already. And the vegetable patch is on the left, also mostly harvested. The orchard is through here."

We reached the hedge and went through a wooden gate to an orchard that was easily the same size as the garden and surrounded by the same hedge. Neat rows of fruit trees grew on two sides of a straight gravel path that led to a back gate, all nicely pruned and with plenty of room between them. The lawn was recently mowed.

"Plums and cherries have already been picked. Pears and late harvest apples aren't ripe yet. So today we'll concentrate on those two trees bearing an early variety that's ready to be picked."

We set out to work. Believe it or not, this wasn't my first time as a harvest labourer. My childhood home had a couple of apple trees in its garden, and as the only child I'd had to help pick them. I'd even had a summer job at a vineyard in France when I was in university, though my memories of that experience were hazy. Mostly because it had been so exhausting that I'd blocked them.

This gig was a holiday compared to that. The pace was leisurely, we had benches and ladders for reaching the top branches more easily, and canvas buckets for the apples hung from our shoulders in harnesses. Kane and I worked on one tree in silence, and Amber and Giselle on another, although Giselle abandoned her wife from time to time to fetch us refreshments.

I had worked with Kane for long enough to find the silence between us companionable. He didn't talk much during ordinary days either. And like he'd promised, this wasn't the first time apple picking for him. He was much faster than I was, and he could reach higher too.

"Here, you take this bucket I just emptied, and I'll go empty yours," he said at one point, standing at the bottom of my ladder and reaching up with his empty canvas bucket.

I removed my almost full one and handed it to him. "Thank you."

He took off a linen newsboy cap he'd donned before we began, and wiped his forehead with the back of his arm. "We're almost done here. Maybe if we hurry, we can finish before lunch."

But Giselle called lunch just then. Kane helped me down from the ladder and we followed Amber out of the orchard, pausing to empty the bucket into a wheelbarrow on our way.

My legs had turned stiff from working on awkward positions, and I shook them as we walked, trying to make the blood circulate again. We reached the gate to the garden and Kane held it open for me, but I gestured him to go through.

"I need to stretch a bit first or I'll fall on my face," I told him, and leaned down to touch my toes.

An arrow struck the gatepost where my head had been a moment before.

~ ~ ~

I NEVER KNEW MY BOSS could move so fast. I'd barely registered the existence of the arrow where one wasn't supposed to be when he had already sprinted halfway down the orchard towards the shooter, keeping behind the trees in case there were more arrows being fired.

Since I was a sitting target—or a bending-over one, which was even worse—I forced my legs to cooperate and ran to take cover behind the nearest tree. The trunk wasn't large enough to cover me completely, but it was better than nothing. My heart was hammering in my chest, but more for the dash than for the attack. Everything had happened so fast that I hadn't had time to be frightened.

Leaning tightly against the tree, I peeked around it to see what Kane was doing. He had reached the back gate out of the orchard and was pressing against the hedge so he could take a similar stealthy look through the opening. His right arm was stretched behind him, as if he was preparing to throw something invisible. As I stared, his fingers curled lightly and blue light glowed in his palm, which then coalesced into a small ball of energy.

He spotted his target and hurled the ball like a cricket bowler over the gate. A distant shriek told it met its mark. He rushed through the gate and disappeared from my sight. Not wanting to miss anything, I ran after him.

There was a common meadow behind the orchard, with well-worn footpaths crisscrossing it. Kane was a few yards down one such path, leaning over a prone form on the ground in eerie imitation of what I'd witnessed behind the shop a week earlier. The only difference was the look on his face. Instead of calm and impassive, he was furious. I'd never seen him this angry before and the effect was unsettling. This wasn't the gentlemanly antiques dealer I worked for. This was a seriously infuriated mage.

I approached them carefully. "Is he…?" I couldn't bring myself to say dead. "…breathing?"

"I'm not in the habit of killing people," he growled, contradicting my memory of the previous attack I'd seen. "He's just unconscious."

I leaned over to take a look. The man was in his late forties, early fifties maybe, and really fit, which I could see clearly as he was wearing a running outfit made of black

Lycra that didn't leave any room for guessing. There was an incredibly technical looking bow next to him, the kind of which you only saw in sports archery, light with all sorts of switches you could tweak.

"He's bleeding though," I said as I noticed a puddle spreading under him.

"Blast."

Kane turned the man carefully to his side. He had fallen on one of his aluminium arrows and it had pierced his side. I squeezed my eyes, nauseous, but Kane wasn't affected.

"It's only a flesh wound," he stated, pulling the arrow off. It came out easily; it was meant for target shooting and not hunting, and had a sharpened tip like a pencil instead of the kind that was meant to stick. Blood spurted out, but he placed his hand above the wound briefly and it stopped.

"We'd better get him into the cottage before he wakes up."

I made to grab the man's legs, but before I had a chance, Kane had already pulled him into a fireman's carry over his shoulders, as if the man didn't weigh anything.

"Take the bow and arrows," he ordered as he headed to the gate. I complied and hurried after him.

We were halfway down the orchard when Amber came to check what was keeping us. She spotted the prone man on Kane's shoulders and hurried to us.

"What's happened?"

"He attacked us and now he's wounded. We need to tend to him immediately," Kane said.

"I'll go prepare."

She swirled around and ran back to the cottage. By the time we reached the kitchen, she and Giselle had already emptied the sturdy table and were busy scrubbing it clean. Kane waited patiently for them to finish, even though the man on his shoulders had to be heavy. Giselle took out a fresh disposable tablecloth from the kitchen cabinet and spread it over the table before he was allowed to place the man there.

I stepped out of the way as she and Amber cut off the tight shirt the man wore. He was still unconscious, and I hoped he would remain that way.

"What caused this?" Amber asked. "Was he shot?"

"It's an arrow wound," Kane explained. "He fell on one of his own arrows."

"It's a flesh wound," Giselle said, poking a gloved finger into the wound. I pressed a hand on my mouth to keep the contents of my stomach in. She noticed it. "Why don't you go have lunch on the patio while we patch this, Phoebe."

"As if I could eat." But I fled to the patio anyway.

Kane followed me there a moment later. I was standing at the edge of the patio, trying to bring my breathing back in control, when I felt him stand next to me.

"I'm not needed in there either." He gestured at the table, where a cold lunch was set. "Let's take a seat."

I agreed, mostly to get off my feet. Now that the situation was over, I didn't entirely trust my legs anymore. He began to fill a plate for himself, but I couldn't eat.

"Will they be able to treat him?"

He gave a reassuring nod. "Yes. Amber is a former trauma nurse."

"I didn't know that." But I could easily imagine it. She had the brusque, no-nonsense manners of one. "I kind of thought they'd heal him with magic."

He smiled. "I wish we could do that, but it's beyond our skills. At best we can nudge the process along a bit, but it's not among any of the talents the three of us have. There are healing potions and salves, but that's just a different form of medicine."

"Then what did you do earlier when you stopped the wound from bleeding?" I made a motion with my hand that imitated his.

"I placed a small shield on it. It merely prevented the blood from flowing, like a bandage would."

I focused on that to keep my mind away from what might be taking place in the kitchen. "So how does your magic work, exactly?"

He stared at the contents of his plate as he pondered the question. "I guess the best way to describe it is molecular manipulation, though we don't call it that. We transform matter into heat or cold, liquid or firm. And then we combine these to create more complex spells."

He made a gesture with his fingers and a small flame appeared on his palm. Another gesture, and it was doused with water appearing from nowhere, which then froze, only to evaporate a moment later. He made it seem so simple and elegant, but I knew it had to be anything but. Anyone could do it otherwise.

Except, he had told me that one had to be born as a mage.

"There's something within you that helps you do this?" I asked, truly curious now.

He shrugged. "Possibly. But don't ask what it is, because there naturally haven't been any genetic studies about what makes us different."

"Or vampires and werewolves either?" I quizzed him.

He grinned. "If you believe in such things…"

I groaned, aggravated, and he laughed.

"I'm sorry you got dragged into this," he then sad, genuine concern in his eyes. "That was never my intention."

His apology warmed me, but I brushed it away. "It's not your fault. If this person wanted to curse you and not your employees, they should've delivered the packet to your home and not your place of business."

He startled. "You know, I hadn't thought of it that way. So why did they?"

I poured myself a glass of fresh apple juice and took a sip. The sharp and sweet taste revived me a little. "Maybe they don't have your home address?"

"It's not exactly a secret among mages," he said, then gave it a thought. "Though I guess it should be, if these sorts of things will become more commonplace."

"You'd have to move to make it secret again."

He grimaced. "Not exactly what I want. I'm fond of my current home."

"Well, perhaps your attacker doesn't know where you live," I consoled him. "Did you recognise him?"

He resumed eating. "No. And more to the point, I don't think he's a mage."

"How can you tell?" I asked, amazed. "Do you people have an aura or something?" He had known that Amelia wasn't a mage just by talking with her.

He nodded. "In general, we can detect it, but not when a person is unconscious. But I doubt he would've used a bow if he were able to use magic."

"Good point."

I was about to ask more when a tall figure in all black entered the garden from the orchard.

Twelve

I TENSED FOR A MOMENT, BEFORE I recognised her. Ashley.

"Where is he?" she growled the moment she was close enough, her face tight. "I swear I only lost him for a second and he was gone. Then I had to wake up Luca, and that took forever at this time of day, and then I had to wait for him to locate the bastard's car. And guess where it led? Straight to here. So where is he?"

"Who?" I asked, baffled. "And how could Luca tell?"

"Never mind, I can smell him," she said, and walked into the kitchen, only to jump back in horror. "Whoa. What happened to him?"

"Who is he?" Kane asked, rising up, alarmed, but I'd already figured it out.

"Mr Spencer." Not what I had expected.

"What happened?" Ashley demanded to know again.

"He tried to shoot Kane with a bow, only to fall on one of his own arrows when Kane retaliated."

Her mouth fell open. Then her upper lip curled and I could swear her incisors lengthened. "I'll end him," she said, but Kane lifted a hand to calm her.

"That won't be necessary. Moreover, I need to ask him questions, like who sent him and how did he know we were here."

I hadn't even come to think of the latter. "There must be someone keeping an eye on your every move."

"I'll go check the perimeter," Ashley stated, and proceeded to do so without delay. Kane resumed his lunch and I'd recovered enough to follow suit. She returned before we were finished.

"There's no one around that I could detect," she told us, taking a seat at the table too, and filling a plate. "Did you tell anyone you'd be here?"

He shook his head. "Who would I have told?"

That sounded kind of sad.

"Perhaps they've planted a tracking app on your mobile," I suggested. He patted his pockets and shook his head.

"I forgot it home."

I couldn't imagine how that was even possible.

"Can they track you with magic?"

His eyes tightened as he gave it a thought. "Maybe. But it's more probable that they tracked you."

"Me?" I squealed in shock.

"They're tracking the curse."

"So they would know I'm the one cursed and not you?" The mere notion made me queasy. He cocked a pointed brow.

"Why else would he have aimed at you?"

I could only stare at him. "I thought he aimed at you. Why would he want to kill me?"

He gestured with his hand. "Because you weren't supposed to be cursed? Perhaps the only way to break the curse is to kill you."

Hexing the Ex

My stomach turned sour. I tried really hard to keep the contents in but I lost the fight. I barely managed to run to the hedge before throwing up the excellent lunch I'd just had.

Giselle was on the patio when I returned. She took one look at my sickly pale face and headed back to the kitchen. Moments later, she returned with a mug of one of her special teas.

"Here. This'll settle your stomach."

I took the mug, but I shook my head. "I doubt tea will work on this kind of shock."

She placed a hand on my shoulder. "What happened?"

Kane answered for me. "I told her that I think Mr Spencer tried to kill her and not me."

"That would do it." Her lips pressed into a tight line. "Well, you can ask for yourselves. He's awake."

The kitchen was mercifully cleaned up after the emergency surgery, and Mr Spencer was seated at a kitchen chair, wearing an old jumper that had to be hot in this weather, but at least he didn't have to sit there bare-chested. He looked bit older than my initial estimate, although it could be because he was pale and probably a little in pain. There were no obvious restraints on him, but he didn't seem to be able to move his arms and legs. He watched us from under his brows.

Kane pulled out a chair and took a seat opposite the prisoner. "Mr Spencer, I presume."

"I don't know who that is," the man stated defiantly.

Kane gave him a level look. "You're not exactly a master spy." That drew snickers from the audience. "We had you tracked from your house to here. So why don't you tell us why you tried to shoot Miss Thorpe."

He gestured at me and Mr Spencer startled. "I wasn't aiming at her."

"Then you're a bad shot," Kane said.

An indignant flush banished the paleness from Mr Spencer's face. "I happen to be a former Olympic-level archer. I'm an excellent shot. Not that I needed to be with the arrows I had."

Kane leaned forward. "What do you mean?"

"You wouldn't understand," Mr Spencer said evasively, and Kane sneered.

"Try me."

"Fine. They were spelled to hit a person who is cursed." The look in his eyes challenged Kane to deny the existence of magic and curses, but it was wasted on my boss.

"By whom?" he only asked.

"By me," Mr Spencer claimed, making Kane snort in derision.

"Hardly. Otherwise, you would've known that Miss Thorpe is the one with the curse."

Mr Spencer frowned. "No, it can't be. I delivered the packet to Mr Kane."

The man definitely wasn't a master spy if he revealed things this easily.

"I am Archibald Kane. So why did you want to curse me? I'm fairly sure I don't know you."

"I didn't curse anyone," Mr Spencer said, defensive now.

"Then who did?"

"I ... can't tell you."

Kane crossed his arms over his chest and leaned back. "You tried to kill Miss Thorpe. Do you want me to turn this matter over to the police?"

Hexing the Ex

Colour fled from Mr Spencer's face again. "No, I just meant to frighten you a little."

"Funny how my head would've been frightened to death if I hadn't moved at the last second," I growled, unable to keep my anger in.

He shot me a besieging look. "That's not how it was supposed to happen. They told me it would not be lethal."

"They?" Kane asked, but Mr Spencer pursed his lips together and wouldn't answer. "I take it you mean the people who made the targeting spell?"

"Yes," he ground out.

"And sent the curse too?" Kane leaned closer. "You trust people who resort to curses, when they tell you the spell on the arrow is harmless?" The man's face tightened, and Kane sneered. "I take that as a no, then. So who are you working for?"

"I ... don't know their names."

Kane cocked a brow. "I find that hard to believe."

"It's true. I belong to this ... society. Secrecy is at the core of it."

"And what does this society do?"

"Magic."

Kane tensed. "Magic?"

"The leaders can do amazing things," Mr Spencer explained, his face animating like he was a believer in an evangelical event. "And they will teach initiates too."

Kane's fists curled and I partly expected energy balls to appear, but his face didn't reveal any anger. "And what have you learned so far?"

"Nothing, but I only recently joined. This operation was supposed to show my commitment to the society."

"And the operation was to deliver the curse, and then kill the recipient?" Kane demanded, his hair starting to billow. Now that I knew about magic, I wondered if it was caused by him and not wind after all.

"No! I told you, I only meant to frighten you."

Kane didn't look convinced. "But you haven't told me why I needed frightening when I was presumably already cursed."

The man had no answer to that, so Kane changed tactics.

"How did you learn about the society?"

Mr Spencer startled. "I was invited by a friend."

"I'm going to need that friend's name."

"Or what?" Mr Spencer asked, lifting his head in a useless act of defiance. Kane sneered.

"The leaders of your society aren't the only ones capable of magic. For example, have you noticed that you're not fastened to that chair with actual ropes?"

Mr Spencer glanced down and his mouth dropped open. He tried instantly to move and couldn't. He began to struggle, but it made no difference.

"I don't believe this," he said, bewildered.

Kane leaned closer. "Yet you believe in magic performed by your leaders? That the arrow was spelled to hit the intended target?"

Mr Spencer pressed his lips together. Kane studied him a moment in silence, before continuing.

"Here's how it's going to go. You will tell me everything about the society, who belongs to it and where you gather. In exchange, we won't go to the police. Trust me, they won't believe in spelled arrows and you will be arrested for an attempted murder."

"Like that would save me," Mr Spencer said bitterly.

Kane shot him a sharp look. "I take it yours isn't a forgiving society?"

"That's one way to put it. I and my daughter won't be safe if I return after failing this operation." He sounded genuinely frightened, but Kane wasn't moved.

"I suggest you take a holiday somewhere until this blows away then."

"That won't be enough," Mr Spencer said, looking desperate. "You need to protect us."

Kane's jaw tightened. "Then you'll have to tell us who we're protecting you from!"

"All I can tell you is that we have a gathering tonight at the upstairs meeting room of a pub at the Temple."

"And do they know what you look like?"

He shrugged. "I guess. But we wear masks at the meeting."

"Good to know." Kane got up. "Let's get you home, then, where you'll give me the mask and all the details of your meetings so far. In exchange, we'll see you and your daughter to the airport safely."

Mr Spencer looked bewildered. "I can't just leave. I have a business to run, and my daughter has her job."

Not to mention a new boyfriend she probably wouldn't want to leave behind, but I didn't say that aloud.

Kane made a gesture with his hand, releasing Mr Spencer and helping him up. "Then I suggest you make arrangements. Preferably after you've reached safety."

~ ~ ~

KANE, ASHLEY, AND I filed into Mr Spencer's car with him, leaving Giselle and Amber to deal with the apples and the two cars there now was, as Ashley had driven there in Amber's small Nissan while tracking Mr Spencer. Kane was behind the wheel, with Ashley sitting at the back with the prisoner. That left me the front seat.

The entire situation felt absurd; being shot at and taking a prisoner, not to mention secret societies that were willing to kill people. Kane looked calm though, as if he dealt with situations like this often. Maybe he did. Maybe mages were unruly in general.

I couldn't ask him though. Despite being aware of magic, I had a notion that Mr Spencer wasn't even as much in the know as I was, and I didn't want to vex my boss by bringing it up. But the silence in the car was getting uncomfortable, so I had to break it somehow.

"Your daughter tells us you're in the wine import business?"

I couldn't believe how much I sounded like my mother just now. For all I resented her attempts to make me a society wife, some lessons had clearly stuck.

Mr Spencer perked, glad to be talking about something else. "Yes. Mostly from smaller vineyards in South France."

"Ah! Which ones? I worked on one there a few years ago." I told the name of the place, which turned out to be one of his suppliers, and we spent most of the ride talking about wine as if this was a perfectly normal situation.

But as we approached his house, the tension in the car returned. "Is your daughter home?" Kane asked Mr Spencer, who shook his head.

"I have no idea. She's a grown woman who doesn't have to tell me where she goes." He grimaced. "How am I supposed to make her come with me?"

"Maybe you should've thought of the consequences before you started shooting people," Ashley growled.

"I thought it was just to intimidate Mr Kane," he said, pulling as far away from her as the back seat allowed.

Hexing the Ex

"You still haven't told us why Mr Kane needs intimidating," I pitched in.

He shrugged. "He would prevent our society from teaching magic."

Kane tilted his head in acknowledgement. "Now that I know your society exists, I will. But it doesn't really matter. Magic cannot be taught."

"Of course it can," Mr Spencer huffed. "My friend has learned amazing things."

"Then your friend was born with the ability and is only now learning to use it. You, however, don't have it," Kane said remorselessly. Mr Spencer's face hardened.

"I don't believe you."

"Then you're wasting your time."

He pulled over on the driveway of Mr Spencer's house and we exited the car. Mr Spencer's hands were bound by magic in front of him, but just in case he thought to run, Ashley walked him into the house.

"Amelia, are you home?" he called once we were in.

"In the kitchen!"

We followed Mr Spencer to the back of the hallway and through a door on the left to a fairly vast and modern kitchen. A sickeningly domestic sight met my eyes. Amelia and Troy were side by side at the stove, cooking together. Troy looked like he was enjoying himself and like he knew what he was doing, even though the whole time we were dating he wouldn't step inside a kitchen.

They both turned to look when we entered and their happy smiles froze. "Dad, what's going on?"

Thirteen

"I'M AFRAID I'M IN A SPOT of a trouble, darling," Mr Spencer told his daughter. "We need to leave home for a while."

"Leave home?" Then she realised Ashley was restraining him. "What are you doing? Release my father immediately."

"Nope." Ashley guided Mr Spencer to sit at the kitchen table, remaining by his side.

"Phoebe, is this your doing?" Troy demanded. He wrapped an arm around Amelia's shoulder in comfort.

I shot him a disgusted look. "No, it's entirely Mr Spencer's doing. He tried to kill me."

"Kill? Don't be absurd," Amelia huffed, turning to her father. "Right, Dad?" But Mr Spencer grimaced and hung his head. Amelia staggered towards Troy. "Dad?"

"I'm afraid your father has become involved in dealings he should know nothing about," Kane said. "And apparently the people he is involved with aren't forgiving. So I suggest you figure out a place to lay low in for a week or so until this blows over."

"A week?" Amelia exclaimed. "I can't go away for a week. I'll lose my job."

"Better that than losing your life," Ashley said dryly.

Amelia snorted in derision. "Surely you're exaggerating."

"You believe your father isn't capable of harming anyone, yet these people managed to make him shoot at me with an arrow," I said. "They won't hesitate to hurt all of you for his failure."

She paled as the truth of my words sank in. "I … can I call my boss?"

"I suggest you only call them after you're safely out of the country," Mr Kane said.

I took out my phone like the good assistant that I was. "So, let's see where we can get you on a short notice."

"Maybe South France," Mr Spencer suggested hopefully. "I've been meaning to visit the suppliers this fall anyway."

I didn't tell him that it was probably the first place these people would look for him, if they knew him well, and just started searching.

"I can get you on a Eurostar to Marseille, but it leaves in a little over an hour and it takes almost that long to drive to St Pancras, so we'd better hurry up."

"Book it," Mr Spencer said.

"For two or three?" I asked, glancing at Troy, who grimaced and lifted his hands in front of him, as if warding me off.

"I'm sorry, but leave me out of this."

"What, your job is more important than supporting the love of your life?" I sneered, but I booked for two without delay.

"How would you know about that?" Amelia demanded. "How do you know Troy?"

I gave her a sweet smile. "Don't worry. I wasn't the love of his life. Otherwise he wouldn't have cheated on me the entire time we dated."

With that, I followed Mr Spencer out of the kitchen so that he could fetch his credit card for me to pay the tickets with. I could hear Amelia demand explanations from Troy behind me. Maybe I didn't need a curse to ruin things for him after all.

I grimaced. I'd become that woman, the one who sought revenge. I didn't even love Troy anymore. What did it matter who he was dating?

But I didn't return to the kitchen to help the two patch things up.

In surprisingly short order, we had the Spencers back in the car, with Kane behind the wheel and Amelia and I in the back with Troy. They hadn't broken up and he had promised to drive the car back to Mr Spencer's house, so he'd had to come too, but I had to sit between the two because they weren't currently speaking.

It was the second most uncomfortable ride of my life.

Sunday afternoon traffic through London was mercifully light, so we reached the train station with time to spare. Troy took the car with perfunctory goodbyes from Amelia and then Kane and I escorted her and Mr Spencer to the train.

"I'll let you know when it's safe to return," he promised Mr Spencer. "And I've placed a spell on you both that prevents you from telling anyone where you are. But don't go calling your friends or family, because that's where they'll look for you first. You'll be putting them in danger too. And before you go, I need the name of your friend who introduced you to the organisation."

A fond look rose on his face. "Ah, yes. She's actually a woman I've been dating recently. Please, be gentle with her," he pleaded.

"As long as you don't contact her, she should be safe. The name?"

"Danielle Mercer."

Kane staggered as if hit, but Mr Spencer didn't notice, because he'd already turned to head to his compartment. The door closed with a hiss and the train began to pull away from the station. We stared after it until it was well and truly gone. Then I turned to Kane.

"I trust you recognised the name? Is she one of your competitors to lead the Council of Mages?"

"Worse," he ground out. "She's my ex-wife."

~ ~ ~

A QUEASY SENSATION SPREAD from my stomach to my bones, freezing them. "I … had no idea you've been married," I managed to say as I followed him out of the station to a mercifully short taxi queue. We got into a cab and were on our way before I'd recovered from the revelation.

I couldn't explain why the news that he had been married was such a shock to me. Maybe because it didn't fit the image of a loner I'd formed of him. Or maybe it was because he'd been married to someone who might be trying to harm him.

"I take it the divorce wasn't amicable?"

His sneer was bitter. "You could say that." Then he startled. "You mean, you think she sent the curse?"

"Of course she did." I barely refrained from rolling my eyes. "Who else could it be, now that we know there's a personal connection to you? She is a mage, right?"

Hexing the Ex

He sighed and rubbed his eyes. "She is. And I guess you're right. I was so sure it was a competitor that a personal motive didn't even occur to me."

"Hell hath no fury and so forth," I said, trying to lighten his mood, but he only grimaced.

"I was the one scorned, and besides, we divorced almost a decade ago."

"That's a long time to wait to retaliate."

He nodded. "So maybe it's not personal after all, but for the reason Mr Spencer said: to prevent me from putting an end to their society."

"It's an illegal enterprise?" I asked, glancing at the driver in case he was paying attention to what we were saying. The plastic partition only blocked so much. "So how would she become involved?"

Kane glanced at the driver too, then lowered his voice. "We're not allowed to reveal magic to humans. It's one of the unbreakable rules we have. Danielle and I disagreed about it during our marriage, so I guess it's not that odd that she'd belong to such a society."

"Yet she pretends not to know magic?"

Mr Spencer had told us that his "friend" had learned amazing things, but the only way that would be possible was if she'd pretended not to know any magic in the first place.

Kane looked pained. "It would seem so. But I can't understand why she would."

"Perhaps you should call her and ask," I suggested lightly, but he staggered in horror.

"I am not doing that."

I turned to face him on the seat. "Oh, come on. We have to get the curse lifted. If she placed it, she can break it."

He put a hand in front of him, warding me off. "I haven't been in touch with her since we divorced. I don't know where she lives, or her phone number, or where she works even." He shook his head. "Besides, I'm not entirely sure it was her. She may have made my life a living hell, but she's not the kind to try to harm anyone."

People change, but I kept the thought to myself, as the notion clearly distressed him.

"But she's involved with the society, so she must know who placed the curse."

"Not necessarily," he instantly countered. "She could be an ordinary member like Mr Spencer."

I shook my head. "No, she has to be much higher up. I think she's one of the leaders, if not the leader, and has a scam going on with the organisation. She lures people into believing they can learn magic and then hooks them so they can't leave."

"To what end?" he asked, disbelieving.

I spread my arms. "I have no idea. Money, power, the usual? They forced Mr Spencer to commit a crime. I bet they would've blackmailed him for it."

His mouth tightened. "I need to think about it."

"Don't think too long. We have their meeting to infiltrate tonight."

He was instantly more animated. "You are not coming!"

"We went through this once already," I said, aggravated. "I'm not staying behind when it concerns me."

"If you're right, these people have a high-stakes con going on. They won't just let you walk in on their meeting, even with a mask on." He waved the mask Mr Spencer had given him. "They've already tried to kill you once."

I jutted my chin up. "Then I'll stay downstairs at the pub and keep an eye on people who come in."

He pointed a finger at me. "Fine, but you'll take Ashley and Luca with you."

"I was planning to."

We reached the shop and he paid the fare. He walked to his car that was parked in front of it. "I'd better go prepare for the evening. I'll return shortly and then we'll go through the plan together."

"You'd better, or I'll make a wish," I threatened him, making him smile.

"You wouldn't curse me. I'm your boss, and you love your job too much to compromise it."

I did, dammit.

"Then you'd better sort things out with your ex before this gets out of hand."

"Like you did with yours?" he quizzed.

My smile was vicious. "Exactly."

He shook his head. "You seem like such a nice person that I would never have thought you have such a mean streak in you."

"If it's any consolation, I didn't know I had it in me either."

With that, I rounded the building to enter through the back door, as the shop was closed.

Ashley had made it home already. She was in the kitchen with Amber and Giselle—and a ton of apples. Sweet scent filled the room, making my mouth water, and I'd already eaten a few when we were picking them.

"You'll never guess who sent the curse!"

Kane probably wouldn't want everyone to know, but this was too important not to share. They paused what they were doing, faces full of curiosity.

"The former Mrs Archibald Kane."

"Oh, great, the bitch is back," Giselle sighed.

"You know her?"

She put down the peeler and the apple she'd been holding. "Unfortunately, yes."

I took a seat at the table and leaned eagerly forward. "Spill."

"Fine, but you'll peel apples while I talk."

I was given a peeler of my own and a bowl of apples and I set to work, though my attention was mostly on Giselle.

"First, you have to understand that Danielle and Archibald come from old and distinguished mage families. There aren't many of us to begin with, and it's seldom that people are at marital age at the same time, so we mostly marry out. Danielle is two years older than Archibald, but that's nothing."

I nodded. It probably also meant that he wasn't born in the nineteenth century after all.

"Everyone always sort of assumed they would marry. They were young, beautiful and gifted. I don't know if their opinion was asked, but during his first year at the university, her third, they fell in love and married soon after he graduated."

I could picture it vividly and didn't like the image. "I've never even asked what he studied," I said. Maybe if I had, I'd learned about his marriage sooner.

"English, if I recall. Or was it history…?" She brushed it aside.

"Never mind. The mage community was ecstatic about the marriage. We had our royal pair who would rise to lead us. All that nonsense. But it soon emerged that they had very different views about magic and our community. Archibald wanted to continue as we'd always done, in secret. She wanted us to come out in the open and lead humans. At first we thought it was just empty talk, but she began to actively work towards it. And then she became interested in the darker side of magic. It began to reflect on their marriage too. Soon they divorced in a spectacular way. She left the country and we thought we'd seen the last of her."

"And now she's back."

Giselle looked unhappy. "I wonder why. She's not eligible to challenge Archibald for the council leadership, if she's still trying to change the direction we're going."

"She belongs to the society that wants to teach humans magic, so I'd say she has some sort of scheme going on."

Amber snorted. "But it's not possible to teach humans magic."

"Which makes me think the endgame is something else entirely," I said, finishing peeling the first apple with flourish. "It could be a means to an end."

"Gather rich and influential people into your organisation and blackmail them into doing your bidding?" Amber asked, getting my meaning immediately. "Pave the way for mages taking over?"

I nodded. "Could be. Why else would they have made Mr Spencer attack us? They believed Kane was already cursed, so killing him would've been … overkill. Blackmail however…"

"If they're willing to resort to curses and murders, we have to stop them," Amber stated, her face grim.

"Not before she's lifted the curse," Ashley said firmly. "I want to get back to work."

"Kane doesn't believe she sent the curse and so won't contact her," I said, frustrated, starting with the next apple. "But he's letting me come with him to the meeting tonight, provided that I stay in the pub and take you and Luca with me."

Ashley nodded. "Good idea. Everyone at the meeting will be masked, but I bet they won't be wearing the masks downstairs. I don't know the faces of most of the mages, but we can take photos."

I jumped up. "Brilliant. I'll go change."

"I'll go wake Luca up." She made to get up too, but Giselle halted us, pointing at us with the peeler for emphasis.

"Neither of you will go anywhere before the apples are peeled."

Fourteen

GISELLE FREED US AN HOUR later. I barely had time to change into inconspicuous pub slash surveillance clothes—all black, naturally—before Kane arrived.

My mind had been occupied with his marriage, so the first thing that came out of my mouth was: "So you're not a hundred and fifty after all."

He pulled back, dismayed. "No. Why would you think that?"

I shrugged. "I don't know, maybe because of your inability to interact with the modern world?"

"Is this about the webpage again?" he asked, annoyed. "Because I allowed you to set one for the shop."

I sketched a flourished bow. "And I thank you for that. But, you know…" I gestured at the black three-piece suit he was wearing again. "This is a bit much for a modern man."

He stared at his clothes. "I like suits. I don't have to think about what to wear."

"And they're perfect for your job," I assured him, not wanting to make him feel bad, although I did have ideas of what he could wear instead. "Besides, it was only after you said that mages live longer that I began to wonder how old you are."

The corners of his eyes crinkled as he smiled. "Well, I'm thirty-five. And unless there's a drastic development in medicine, I won't live to be a hundred and fifty."

Good to know.

"Warlocks, however…"

I lifted my hands to stop him. "I'm not ready for that conversation."

He grinned. "Are you ready for tonight's mission, then?"

I nodded. "I am, as is Ashley. It's Luca I'm not certain about."

The man in question ambled into the kitchen just then, dressed in faded joggers and a rumpled T, his long hair mussed as if he'd only just woken up. "Did I hear my name mentioned?"

"Yes. Get dressed. We're headed to a pub to bust an illegal mage society," I told him, and he grinned.

"Sweet."

"We're not busting anything," Kane said firmly. "We're observing and then reconvening to consider our next step."

"It's still more fun than what I had planned for today," Luca said.

"Laundry?" I quipped.

"Bookkeeping."

I shot him a baffled look. "What do you keep books for?"

As far as I knew, he worked part-time at the shop, which couldn't pay all that much.

Hexing the Ex

"I have my money-making operations," he said, disappearing down the stairs. I glanced at Amber, who shrugged.

"Stocks and online poker. But he's very good at both."

Huh. "I guess there aren't many job opportunities for nocturnal vampires…"

We took Ashley's car because it was largest. Amber came along too. She couldn't participate in our surveillance operation on the off chance that she would be recognised by the other mages, but she would drive the car back so we wouldn't have to waste time looking for parking. We would be cutting it close to the starting time of the meeting as it was.

"So what's the plan?" Luca asked, stretching his arms on the backrest behind Amber and me in the back seat.

He was dressed in crisp blue jeans and a white button-down shirt with the top buttons left open, looking the part of a man heading to a pub for a casual pint.

"I have the mask and passwords from Mr Spencer," Kane said, "as well as the exact time I should arrive, so that I won't be spotted by other members. You three will remain downstairs, and if possible, photograph everyone going up."

"We should've gone there early, because the leaders will likely have arrived before the ordinary members," I noted, and Kane nodded.

"That can't be helped. But you can stay after it ends and hope you'll capture their faces when they leave."

"And what happens if they ask you how your 'scaring' operation went?" Amber asked.

He shrugged one shoulder. "I'll tell them the cursed person remained indoors the whole day and I had no chance to do it."

"What if they recognise you as a mage?" I asked, getting worried.

"I have a spell prepared for a swift flight," he assured me. "However, if they're not hostile, I'll simply ask them to break the curse."

I hoped for all our sakes that it would be that easy. But if it was his ex-wife who'd placed the curse for personal reasons, she might be vicious enough to try to harm him in other ways.

The corner pub near the Middle Temple Gardens was purpose built in 1920s, but its soot-blackened redbrick walls and black-framed, small-paned windows made it look like it had stood there for centuries. The taproom was fairly small and had oaken walls and a bar that looked original, but otherwise the interior was new, though made to appear old.

"Ah, this brings back memories," Luca said with a content sigh as he looked around. He and I came in together, with Ashley having entered earlier and Kane following behind at the exact time Mr Spencer had given him.

"Of what?" I asked curious.

"Of my misbegotten youth at the Honourable Society of Middle Temple."

My jaw dropped. "You're a barrister?" That was not what I would've assumed. "Wait, what do you mean youth? You're my age."

He grinned. "You had your chance to find out how old I am…"

He sauntered to the bar and ordered two pints. The place was fairly full, but we found a ledge at the back near the stairs where we could rest our pints and observe the people going upstairs.

Hexing the Ex

I glanced around and spotted Ashley on the other side of the stairs, at the short end of the bar. There was a gap between her and the men in suits next to her, which made her stand out a little, but then again, her size and bald head didn't exactly help her to blend in.

Her sleeveless T-shirt revealed the strength of her arms, and she'd added a couple of earrings to her right brow to join the ones on her left ear. She was leaning against the bar, holding her phone, to all appearances engrossed with her social media, but I knew she was prepared to take photos.

I took out my phone too. "Stand where you are so that I can use you as a cover when I take photos," I said to Luca.

"Okay, but you'll have to look like you're having a good time, or it'll be bad for my reputation as a ladies' man."

I grinned. "Why don't you entertain me, then."

"Very well. The year was 1926 and this pub was newly opened. I and my fellow pupil Hector Pierce had just survived a vicious interrogation, also known as mid-term exams…"

The story went on forever and involved drunken escapades of two law pupils a century ago, silly and amusing, and I didn't believe a word of it.

While he regaled me with his stories, I photographed everyone who went upstairs. Their faces were bare when they crossed the pub one at a time, but they donned opera masks the moment they were behind the wall. Kane arrived too and he didn't even glance at us, as if he was accustomed to this sort of subterfuge.

I, on the other hand, barely managed not to give him a thumbs-up.

The appointed time for the meeting struck, and I put down my phone, certain that everyone had already arrived. Surely they wouldn't allow late-comers in. Luca took our glasses and turned to head to the bar, when a woman entered the pub.

She paused at the door and everyone turned to look. She let her gaze brush over the taproom, her appraisal cool, the corner of her mouth slightly curled, as if she wasn't impressed by what she saw.

She didn't strike me as the most beautiful woman I'd ever seen, like Amelia had, but if you'd put the two side by side, she would've won, hands down. The men pulled themselves straighter when her eyes met them, and the women instantly fiddled with their hair or clothes. She crossed the floor towards the stairs and everyone parted to give her way.

As she came closer, I saw that she was slightly older than I'd assumed, maybe in her late thirties, with faint lines by her mouth and the corners of her eyes. She was about my height, but with such a dainty body that she appeared smaller. Her face was pleasingly symmetrical, with a sharp chin and lean cheeks. Her slightly downturned green eyes were heavily outlined with black, and her full lips had some gloss, but otherwise her makeup was light. Her hair was rich brown, close-cropped at the back, and longer at the front, where it fell asymmetrically on both sides of her face, giving her an elf-like appearance.

She wore a business pantsuit that became her slender form, and while the cut was fairly masculine, it didn't make her look manly. She oozed such self-confidence and charisma that if she chaired a boardroom, she would definitely get the members do whatever she asked. I was not surprised when she passed us and climbed the stairs, donning a black mask as she went. And I was sure she would be allowed in even if she was late.

"Wow," Luca said, shaking his head, as if waking up from a dream. "I think I'll need a moment by myself."

"Yeah." I wasn't aroused by her, unlike most men there—and some women too—but she had definitely made an impression. "I forgot to take her photo, I was so busy staring."

Luca grinned. "No worries. Kane will recognise her."

It took me a moment to figure out his meaning. Then my heart fell and settled as a cold lump in my stomach. "You mean…?"

"Yep. That was Danielle Mercer, the former Mrs Archibald Kane."

We might be up against a tougher nut than I'd anticipated.

"We'd better hope Kane is truly recovered from their marriage, or she'll walk all over him."

"Good thing we're here to support him," Luca stated, making me snort.

"She'll snap her fingers and you'll roll over like an eager puppy."

He grinned, unapologetically.

We settled down to wait for the meeting to be over. Luca told me more outrageous stories from his long life and I pretended to listen. But my mind was taken by Ms Mercer.

No wonder Kane hadn't remarried, or wasn't even dating anyone. It couldn't be easy to recover from a woman like Danielle Mercer. She was mesmerising, a person who would get whatever she wanted, one way or another, messing with your head and heart as she went for her goal. And now she was back, bent on harming him again.

Not if I had anything to say about it.

"So what does she do for a living?" I asked, interrupting Luca's story, but he didn't need to ask who I meant.

"I have no idea. Let's check her out."

I took out my phone again and made a search. She wasn't on any social media, but we did learn that she was the manager of a luxury hotel by Hyde Park where all the rich and influential people stayed when they visited London.

"That's a great place to be if you're aiming for world domination. She has direct access to great power and wealth," I noted. Luca nodded.

"Maybe I should get a job as a night concierge there and snoop around. See what she's up to."

I gave him a sideways look. "I'm fairly sure a place like that requires a bit more than skill in online poker and a law degree from between the wars."

He grinned. "How do you think I supported myself before the internet?"

There was a time before the internet?

"Then how will you explain to your employer that a bloke in his twenties has fifty years' experience on the job?"

He made a dismissive gesture with his hand. "If I'll apply directly with her, she'll know why."

"But won't that blow your cover?" I was getting a bit worried, but he shrugged.

"She doesn't know who I am. Why would she suspect anything?"

He had a point.

Hexing the Ex

Apart from her official work phone number, there was nothing about her online that we could find. But the hotel website had a couple of photos of her, taken at gala events organised in the hotel. She seemed to be in her element. In one photo she was with Mr Spencer even, and they looked great together. He was only forty-eight—I'd learned when I booked the train tickets—tall and fit. He looked great in evening clothes, and successful enough not to be completely overshadowed by her. He was looking at her with awe, and I felt a twinge in my heart knowing that we would be breaking his before this was over.

Then again, he had tried to kill me. Sod him.

A chat message from Ashley interrupted our search: The barman is giving me the stink eye, saying I'm scaring the customers.

Just order another drink. He won't throw out a paying customer.

Luckily the meeting ended before the barman gathered enough courage to remove her from the premises—and without any incidents that would've resulted in Kane leaving the meeting in haste. One by one, the members came down the stairs, taking off their masks before entering the taproom, Kane among them. But they had a direct line of sight to me and I couldn't take their photos without them noticing. I glanced at Ashley, who didn't have a similar problem, and put my phone away. She could handle the photographing.

In her turn, Danielle Mercer descended the stairs, her mask off. She spotted me and our eyes met. She gave me a cursory glance, sneered lightly, and then ignored me as she passed us. I know I was just a stranger in a pub to her, but her reaction felt oddly personal.

I should've confronted her right there and demanded she remove the curse. With a pub full of people, she couldn't have hurt me with magic. Probably. But I was too intimidated by her to even consider it before she was already out of the door.

Only then did the spell break.

"We should follow her."

Fifteen

LUCA WAS INSTANTLY GAME. "Good idea. Even if she takes a cab, I can track it to her home."

I sent a quick message to Ashley. She promised to follow us once everyone had left the meeting.

Outside the pub, we paused to look around. Danielle turned a corner a little way down the street towards the river, disappearing from our sight.

"At least she didn't take a cab," I said in a low voice as we hurried after her.

She walked calmly along the empty streets, the click of her heels echoing off the walls. I would've been nervous walking there alone at that time of night, but she didn't even glance around. It worked for our advantage, but we kept our distance anyway, in case our steps echoed too, though we'd both worn trainers just for such an occasion.

She reached the end of Arundel Street and crossed Temple Place to the steps down to the Victoria Embankment.

"The entrance to Temple Station is through there," Luca said, and we sped up. We reached the top of the steps just in time to see her enter the tube station and ran after her.

There were more people around than on the street, and we didn't have to be terribly stealthy as we went through the gate—luckily, we'd brought our OysterCards—and followed her down the tunnels towards the correct platform.

"She's taking the District Line west," I noted.

Luca studied the map on the wall. "That's not good. There are several stations along it where she can change lines to practically anywhere in London."

"We'll just have to be vigilant."

We didn't enter the almost empty platform but waited at the mouth of the tunnel to board the train, making sure we were in a different carriage than Danielle.

"Ashley didn't make it on time," I noted as the doors closed and the train pulled away from the station.

"She can find us," Luca assured me.

She'd better. We'd switched off our phones so they wouldn't ring at an inopportune time, so she couldn't contact us, and the phones didn't work underground anyway, so we couldn't call her.

The carriage was empty, but we stood by the door and peered out every time the train pulled into a station to see if Danielle stepped off. But it wasn't until at Earl's Court, eight stations later, that she did. We only waited for her to disappear down the tunnel before hopping off the train and hurrying after her.

She didn't head to the exit, however, but switched to a southbound train. "She can get all the way to Wimbledon on this one," I said. "Good thing I know that neighbourhood. I grew up there."

But we didn't end up there. She disembarked at Putney Bridge station, the last station on the north side of the Thames. It was an over-ground station built above the

Hexing the Ex

streets so that the line could cross the river over a bridge. Open to the elements as it was, there was nothing to hide behind.

It was late, we were the only three people there, and Danielle would have to walk past us to reach the stairs down to the street. She might remember me from the pub and we couldn't have that. Making a snap decision, we hastened down the steps before her, not looking back to see if she was following, and walked resolutely towards the nearest street corner. Only once we'd rounded it did we pause to look where she had gone. My heart was beating fast for the excitement.

"She's headed in the opposite direction," Luca said, and I shuddered.

"I wouldn't take that footpath alone at this time of night."

Luca smiled as he pulled me after Danielle. "When you have access to her level of magic, the darkness ceases to frighten you."

I didn't have that access, so I was grateful for his company as we followed her down the dark path. She turned right at the other end and we ran to the corner of the street to take another peek.

"She seems to be headed towards Hurlingham Park," Luca mused. The name didn't mean anything to me. I just about knew that we were in Fulham, a well-to-do neighbourhood in West London.

"What's there?"

He gave me an incredulous look. "Rugby and polo. The best, most exclusive clubs around."

"Not really my area of interest," I said apologetically. "So why would she go there?"

"It's in the middle of a residential neighbourhood. My guess is she's headed home."

He turned out to be right. There were long rows of two and three storey Edwardian terraces on both sides of the street, all in great repair with expensive cars parked in front of them. Just as the park came into view, Danielle entered a large redbrick end-of-terrace at the corner of two streets.

"Fancy," Luca whistled. "She clearly has money."

I looked around and made a note of the address so that I could tell it to Kane. "So what now?"

"I'm game for snooping around if you are," he suggested.

It was tempting, but I hesitated. "It's not exactly easy."

A brick wall separated the house from the streets on its two sides. We walked down the side street towards the back of the house, only to find that the back yard was separated from the next house by a tall hedge. Hedge grew behind the brick wall too, blocking the view and making it impossible to scale the wall.

A wooden gate wide enough for a car led to the backyard, but the hedge seemed to block it too. That didn't stop Luca from pushing his head through.

"There's a gap for a car here. Let's go."

"I don't know…"

But he'd already hoisted himself over the gate and through the gap. I had no choice but to follow. Good thing I'd dressed for sneaking around.

It wasn't a large yard. Most of it was taken up by a garage, and it was blocked in from all directions by walls, hedges, and fences. The light from the street barely reached there and it was very dark.

"How can you see anything?" I grumbled in a low voice when Luca walked closer to the house as if in daylight. I had to watch every step on the paved path and I still feared I'd stumble.

"Vampires have good night vision."

Right…

He reached a window and peeked in. "It's the kitchen."

Lights came on in there just then and he ducked fast. I froze in the middle of the garden, hoping that the darkness would hide me, my heart beating so fast in fright it was difficult to breathe. I watched Danielle go to the fridge, take out a bottle of water, and head back out, switching off the lights as she went. Relief made my legs watery. I was not built for this sort of excitement.

I was about to call Luca that we would leave, when I saw to my horror that he was already climbing the brick wall of the house like a nimble spider. I held my breath, fearing alternately that he would fall or that he would be discovered, but he reached the next floor windowsill without mishaps.

"It's her bedroom," he said in a low voice. "Maybe I can get in."

But before he could try, the door there opened and light from the hallway flowed in. Last thing I saw before lights came on in the room was Luca dropping back to the ground. I couldn't see him move and I feared the worst, but I couldn't go to him either, because Danielle had clearly noticed something. She came to the window and looked out to the garden. I held absolutely still, and her gaze never reached my spot. It wasn't until she pulled the drapes across the window, blocking the view, that I allowed myself to relax.

My legs had turned stiff and I had to force myself to move. I wanted to head to the street, but I made my way to the house instead. Luca wasn't lying injured on the ground like I'd feared. He was studying the ground floor windows, looking for a way in.

"We're not breaking in," I hissed to him. "We're leaving."

"Relax. I can be really stealthy. What could possibly happen?"

A low growl sounded behind us, making my bones vibrate with primal fear.

~ ~ ~

"DO NOT MOVE," Luca said so silently that I barely heard him.

"What is it?" I mouthed in return, trusting he could read my lips with his superior vampire vision.

"A hellhound."

I almost lost the control of my bladder in shock, and I could swear the growling intensified. "They're not real."

"Vampires aren't real either, yet here I am."

Good point.

"I'm going to stun it. It won't hold it for long, so prepare to run."

I didn't have time to tell him my legs weren't working properly. There was a flash that I felt instead of saw, as there was no light. I heard a thump behind me, but I didn't have time to check what it signified. Luca took my hand and pulled me with him.

"Let's go!"

A surge of adrenaline helped me run across the garden and vault over the gate. Then we were already running down the street. "The station is the other way," I panted.

"We can't lead it to where people are. We're headed to the park."

"Where it can kill us unnoticed?" I shrieked.

I did not like that plan, but as I could already hear the beast coming after us, its nails scraping against the pavement, I wasn't about to turn and head to the opposite direction.

The entrance to the park was locked at that time of night, but the iron gate was low and easily vaulted. There were no lights in the park and the light from the streetlights soon disappeared behind us, but Luca was pulling me down the path with such speed that I had no time to look at what was under my feet.

It was best I didn't think of my feet at all or I'd fall. I was not made for running this fast.

A growl reverberated so close behind me that I could practically feel a hot breath through my clothes. As if drawn by the sound, I glanced behind—and wished I hadn't. The largest dog I'd ever seen was approaching fast. It looked a bit like an English Mastiff, but it was as tall as a pony, with powerful muscles, a huge head, fangs like a predator, and paws the size of a tiger. Saliva was dripping from its mouth, as if it was anticipating a delicious meal. Its size made it a bit slow, but powerful. It wouldn't tire. There was absolutely no way we could outrun it.

"Can't you stun it again?"

Luca glanced over his shoulder, grimaced, and without slowing down, threw an energy ball at the hellhound. It met its mark, but it barely slowed the beast. Luca sped up and somehow managed to make me run faster too.

An outdoors gym came into view, lit even at that time of night, and he pulled me there. "Quick, climb up that jungle gym," he said, throwing me halfway up with such force that I almost missed the bar and fell. Luckily, he hadn't let go of me yet, and he managed to pull me up after him as he climbed. The beast's jaws snapped at my feet a fraction too late.

It was one of those contraptions meant for exercising, not for children's amusement: a half dome about two metres at its peak made of thick iron bars half a metre apart horizontally and vertically, with absolutely nothing to rest on. We climbed to the top and perched on our stomachs over the bars, our legs held high as the beast leaped after us. It was so large that it couldn't fit between the bars, and it couldn't find purchase on them either to climb after us. That didn't stop it from lunging at us again and again. Luca kept bombarding it with energy balls, but they barely slowed it.

"That thing can go on longer than I can conjure these," he said, panting a little. "And if it doesn't give up before morning, I'm screwed."

I looked around for a way out—and froze in newfound fear. A wolf half the size of the hellhound was standing on the other side of the jungle gym, its hackles up, and a vicious snarl on its face. We were trapped.

I let out a frightened mewl that made Luca look at where I was pointing. To my amazement, he relaxed and grinned. "Good, the cavalry is here."

Before I could comprehend his meaning, the wolf attacked the hellhound. A frightening battle of teeth and claws ensued, made more terrifying because it was almost silent. I watched in mesmerised horror as the wolf pummelled the hellhound, biting and scratching, getting its hide bitten in return. It was smaller, but it was more determined. Sooner than I would've thought possible, the wolf had the beast's throat between its jaws.

Hexing the Ex

It bit down—and the hellhound was no more.

Literally. The moment life left its body, it disappeared, fading into nonexistence like a bad special effect in an old TV series. The wolf slumped, breathing heavily. Blood was oozing out of a gash on its side.

Luca climbed nimbly down and kneeled by the wolf. It snarled, but Luca lifted up his hands in a calming gesture. "It's me. I'll just take a look."

I was slower to follow, both because my legs wouldn't obey me and because I was frightened to death of the wolf. Just because it wasn't immediately attacking us didn't mean it wouldn't. It kept growling in a low voice as Luca went over its wounds.

"You'll live," he declared, just as I reached ground. "Now, let's get you home."

"Home?" I screeched.

He grinned. "Surely you recognise her?"

How could he be so calm? We'd just barely escaped a hellhound, only to watch it being killed by this beast. But since he kept pointing at the wolf, I took a closer look.

It was larger than a normal wolf, grey with thick fur that had suffered somewhat for the fight. One of its ears was slightly torn, and the other one…

"Are those earrings?"

A row of them lined the edge of the large, pointy ear, almost disappearing in the fur. I leaned closer. I recognised those earrings. My heart jumped.

"Is she … Ashley?"

"Yep."

"She is a werewolf?"

He looked amused. "You didn't believe her?"

"Of course I didn't bloody believe her." I still wasn't willing to believe, even though I could see it with my own eyes. But we couldn't leave her here.

"So how do we get her home? Can she shift back or something?" I looked around as if transportation would materialise out of thin air.

Luca shook his head. "I'm not sure she has energy for it. Plus, she'd be naked."

"Might cause an even bigger stir than a huge wolf," I said dryly, and he tilted his head in agreement.

"We'd best call backup."

I took out my phone, switched it on and selected Giselle's number. "Can you pick us up?" I said the moment she answered. "And bring your van."

Sixteen

By the time Giselle arrived, Luca had located Ashley's clothes and other belongings under a shrubbery nearby. Ashley had recovered enough to walk, though her going was tottery even on four legs, and she still wouldn't shift.

I hadn't told Giselle why we needed the van. Her eyes grew large when she spotted Ashley, but she didn't comment and simply opened the back doors so the wolf could climb in. I placed the clothes next to her, just in case she felt like becoming a human again during the ride. Then we climbed to the front next to Giselle.

"So what happened?" she asked the moment she had the car running.

Luca and I glanced at each other. "Nothing," we said in unison, and then burst out laughing. Mine was definitely hysterical.

It was a little over a seven-mile drive across the town and it went fast at that time of night. I'd barely pulled myself back together when we reached home. Ashley hadn't shifted yet, but at least her wounds had closed. We let her out and into the house and she headed to her room with a click of her nails on the polished hardwood stairs.

I followed more slowly, barely having energy to get to the kitchen, where I was in for a surprise. Kane.

"Where the hell have you been?" he demanded, rising up to meet us. He looked truly angry. "It's been hours and you haven't answered your phone."

It hadn't even occurred to me he hadn't headed straight home from the meeting. "I'm sorry. I switched it off so it wouldn't ring and ruin our spying."

"Spying?"

"We followed your ex-wife home," I said, proud of our initiative, but it only made him angrier.

"That was really reckless of you. What if she had noticed you? She's dangerous."

"She didn't," I assured him. "And on the plus side, we now know where she lives."

He wasn't impressed. "And the downside?"

I grimaced. "We kind of killed her hellhound."

He staggered and barely made it to a chair before collapsing. "No…"

"Well, Ashley did," I amended, baffled by his reaction. "I couldn't even run fast enough to escape it. Luca had to drag me with him." I flashed the vampire a grateful smile and he grinned back.

Kane wasn't listening. He had covered his mouth with a hand, as if warding off nausea, his eyes closed. Giselle placed a mug of her special tea on the table next to him.

"Drink this. It'll help."

But he didn't touch it.

"What's the matter?" I asked, getting worried. "You said yourself that mages are guarded by hellhounds."

"Mages aren't," he said, pulling himself together with effort. "Only warlocks are able to summon them."

Hexing the Ex

"Warlocks?" I didn't immediately catch his meaning, but then I wanted to sit down and curse too. My mind raced frantically to find an explanation that wouldn't upset him.

"Perhaps it wasn't her hellhound. Perhaps a warlock lives in the same building and it belonged to them."

But he shook his head, looking grim and sad. "I have to face the truth. She's not the woman I once loved."

I'll say.

He rose. "I'd best head home. I'll see you tomorrow." He patted me on the shoulder as he passed me. "I'm glad you're safe."

The moment he disappeared down the stairs, I collapsed in exhaustion. "This day has been a year long."

Giselle gave me the mug Kane had ignored. "Drink this. You'll sleep better."

I took the mug and drank thirstily. I needed all the help I could get to recover from the day. But I wasn't ready for bed yet. "Shouldn't we go through the photos we took at the pub? See if you recognise anyone?"

"Let's go down to my lair. I'll upload the photos to my computer and make a facial search," Luca said.

The mere thought of climbing two flights of stairs down and back again exhausted me, but I pushed myself up anyway. Giselle lifted her hands up, halting us.

"There's time for that tomorrow. You need to rest now."

Grateful for her intervention, I headed to my room. I was too wound-up to sleep, but Giselle's tea worked its wonders again, and I didn't stir the whole night. I woke up rested and ready to face the world.

Ashley exited the bathroom in human form just as I came out of my room. She was wearing only a sports bra and knickers, so I could see all the bruises decorating her body. The wound in her side had mostly healed, but a horrendous scar was still visible, and she looked like she was having the worst hangover of her life.

"Thank you for saving my life last night," I said after a brief awkward pause. I wanted to reach for a hug, but even in this form she didn't exactly look like she would welcome it.

She grinned. "No problem. It's been too long since I was in a good fight."

I shook my head, amazed that she would see it that way. I'd been frightened out of my mind.

"If you hadn't arrived when you did…" I shuddered. "How did you find us?"

"I followed your scent," she stated, as if it was the most natural thing in the world.

"We took the tube."

She nodded. "I did too. I took a good sniff every time the doors of the train opened to see if you'd exited it. There was so little traffic that it actually worked, except at Putney Bridge Station, where the open air was messing with the scent trail. But I managed to catch it." She made a sweeping motion with her hand. "From there it was easy to follow you. And good thing I did. Where the fuck did you find the hellhound anyway?"

"It was guarding Danielle Mercer's home."

She grimaced. "That's not good."

"So she's definitely a warlock?" Kane's upset had made me hope otherwise.

"Yeah…" She rubbed her face. "I'd best get back to bed. It takes a toll to shift and heal when the moon isn't full."

Hexing the Ex

She shuffled to her room and I went to the bathroom to prepare for the day.

Kane was in the kitchen when I got there, looking perfectly put-together in his three-piece like always, a cup of tea in front of him.

"What are you doing here?" I asked, baffled.

He smiled. "Good morning to you too. It occurred to me that we didn't really get to talk last night. I was too shocked by your news. But I have time now."

I took a seat and Giselle put a full plate in front of me. "So how did the meeting go?" I asked as I began to do justice to Giselle's breakfast. "Any trouble?"

He gestured vaguely with his hand. "It was amazingly uneventful. No one spoke to me. No one spoke with anybody. They didn't even ask about the operation. The whole setup seemed fairly amateurish, so I don't understand why Mr Spencer was so afraid of them."

I took a reviving sip of coffee. "What did you do?"

"There was a rollcall and then one man was accepted as a full member. There was an initiation rite that was fairly ridiculous and involved a lot of showy magic, and then we left." He looked so disappointed that I had to pat him on the arm.

"It's better than the opposite. The aim was to identify the participants anyway."

I took out my phone and began to show the photos to him. Twenty people had attended, most of them men. Kane kept shaking his head, not recognising anyone. Giselle and Amber weren't any help either, so we assumed they were the human members of the organisation.

"I didn't stay to the end," I confessed, "so I didn't get the faces of the leaders. They're in Ashley's phone."

Amber went to fetch it and we began anew. It wasn't until we reached the last photos of the people leaving that the three of them perked.

"That's Anthony Eaton," Giselle said, and Kane frowned.

"He must have been the one who led the ceremonies. I thought I recognised the spellcasting style. But what's he doing with these people?"

"Is he your competitor?" I asked and he shook his head.

"No. He's a fairly low-level mage, skill-wise. He won't ever be more than rank and file."

"Those are usually the easiest to lure to an operation like this," Amber noted. "It gives them a sense of importance."

"Maybe he's the one who started the organisation. He did lead the proceedings," Kane suggested.

I gave him a slow look. "Have you met your ex-wife? That woman is not a follower, and definitely not of weaker men."

He grimaced. "I guess…" He lifted his cup to his mouth and glanced at me from the corner of his eyes. "So where does she live?"

I wasn't fooled by his attempt at nonchalance. This mattered to him.

"In Fulham. And she runs the Westbourne Hotel in Kensington. She's been there two years already."

His brows shot up. "Two years? And I had no idea she was in London." He flipped the photos on Ashley's phone and Danielle's picture came up. He paused and studied it for a long time, but I couldn't read his face. Was he wistful? Hoping for a reunion? Angry? "I can't believe she has become a warlock."

Hexing the Ex

I could. An ambitious woman who constantly ran into a glass ceiling could become all kinds of frustrated and angry. The mage community was probably as sexist as the human one. If she had a way around it—or through it—she might take it.

"What about these other people?" I asked to distract him.

Amber took the phones. "I'll upload these to Luca's computer. He can do a facial search for them when he wakes up."

"And this Eaton fellow?"

"I'll deal with him," Kane said.

We finished our breakfast in silence. I fetched my phone from Luca's room—he wasn't sleeping in a coffin but spread-eagled on his large bed, completely out of it—and then we headed to work with Kane.

Monsieur André was waiting outside the gallery door.

"Bugger. You deal with him." Kane practically pushed me towards him.

"Oh come on…" But I plastered on a smile and spread my arms in welcome. "Monsieur André! What a pleasant surprise. What brings you here so early on a Monday morning?"

"None of that Monsieur André stuff, thank you," he said firmly. "I'm done with that nonsense. It's Andrew."

My heart sank. "Surely you haven't stopped painting?"

This was my fault.

"Of course not. But I'm more focused now. In everything." He looked like it too. His eyes were bright and alert, he was cleanly shaven and nicely groomed, and though he was still dressed in all black, there was nothing odd about the jeans and T-shirt combo. "I quit smoking and broke up with my boyfriend who wasn't supportive enough and only wanted money. And I've figured out how to hang the paintings."

"That's good news," I said feebly. I pointed at the gallery window, where a decal with Monsieur André's name advertised the exhibition. "Should we change that?"

"No need. I'll make the announcement of my new name at the opening."

I sighed in relief. The company where we bought the window decals probably would've been able to do new ones by Thursday, but it was better that we didn't have to change them.

"Would you care for tea before we start?"

He brushed my offer aside. "No time. I have a meeting with a new publicist in two hours."

Okay…

Kane disappeared upstairs to his office, the bastard, and I led Andrew to the gallery. He pulled out a sheet of neatly folded paper from his pocket and unfolded it.

"I've made a floor plan."

And we followed it to the letter. In no time at all, we had all the paintings where he wanted them to be. It was refreshing after the previous week's indecision, and I couldn't entirely feel sorry for what I'd done.

I wondered about the curse as I climbed upstairs after he left. It was so random and rather ineffective. If Danielle wanted to hurt Kane, why had she chosen such an odd one? What could she possibly think to achieve with having him curse random people? Especially since one could wish people well too.

Come to think of it, why had she believed that he would trigger the curse? He had recognised it for what it was the moment he saw it.

And then it hit me.

Seventeen

"DANIELLE DIDN'T MEAN TO CURSE you," I declared as I entered Kane's office. He lifted his gaze from the computer monitor and gave me a baffled look.

"Who else would she want to curse?"

"Me."

He straightened in his chair. "What on earth for? She doesn't even know you."

"I don't mean me personally." I plopped myself on the guest chair, exhausted from lugging the heavy paintings around all morning. "Any non-mage working for you. We would open the packet for you and likely trigger the curse. I bet she counted on me accidentally cursing you the first thing, only I fainted instead."

"I guess that makes sense. More sense anyway than that she would believe I would accidentally trigger the curse." He rummaged his desk to locate his mobile phone. "We need to talk with Anthony Eaton. Ask him about the curse."

"Not Danielle?"

He shuddered. "I'm not ready to face her yet. Tony is the weak link. He'll talk." But instead of placing a call, he got up. "We'd best make a surprise visit."

"We?"

A slow smile spread on his face. "I can learn, you know."

I decided not to gloat. I just smiled brightly and followed him out. Instead of taking his car, Kane hailed a taxi on Oxford Street and we drove three miles south across the busiest part of London. I hadn't caught the address when Kane gave it to the driver, and so was taken by a surprise.

"The Houses of Parliament?" I exclaimed when the cab stopped to let us out. "He's not an MP, is he?"

The corner of his mouth quirked. "No, a fiscal clerk for the Commons."

"An accountant?" Not exactly what I'd imagined, but if Danielle wanted world domination, a person close to the MPs would do as a henchman. "So how do we get in? Do you wave your hand and they forget we're here?"

He gave me a slow look. "This is not Star Wars, and we're not able to manipulate minds, no matter how weak."

"You've seen Star Wars?"

He shook his head, exasperated, and led me to the visitors' entrance, where we had to queue in after a group of school children, fill in forms, prove our identity, and get through a metal detector. By the time we were through, Anthony Eaton was waiting for us, summoned there by security. So much for the element of surprise.

He was in his fifties, with thinning hair, slouching shoulders, and a dull beige suit. Nervous sweat was beading on his forehead.

Hexing the Ex

"Archibald! What brings you here?" he asked with a forced cheerfulness, coming to shake Kane's hand. "And with such a lovely companion too." He nodded at my direction, but he didn't really look at me.

Kane smiled affably. "Miss Thorpe is my assistant. Is there anywhere we can talk?"

"Have you had lunch yet? We have an excellent canteen here."

It was a bit early for lunch for us, but we weren't about to decline a chance to dine at the Palace of Westminster. He led us through the cathedral-like hall to a side door where narrow stairs took us a floor down. I'd visited the place a couple of times with school, so I managed not to gawp. Much.

The grandeur was reserved for the public areas. Below ground the hallways were bland, with concrete floors and plain walls. The canteen where Mr Eaton led us was for the support staff, a windowless, low-ceilinged room with rows of tables and plastic chairs. The food line was at the other end. It looked a bit industrial, but the scents were delicious.

There was no queue, so we selected our food and Kane paid for everyone; not a great expense, as the meals were heavily subsidised. We chose a table at the side of the room and sat down. There were no people near us, but I nevertheless wondered why we were having the talk in public. Anyone might overhear us.

As if reading my mind, Kane made an elaborate gesture with his hand and the noises in the room disappeared. "There. Now we can talk in peace."

Perspiration appeared on Mr Eaton's upper lip. "Oh? This is something serious, then?"

"I attended your meeting last night," Kane said without preamble. Mr Eaton froze.

"I ... don't know what you're talking about."

Kane didn't heed his denial. "You were photographed leaving. You know it's illegal what you're doing with that society. I could get the council to expel you."

Mr Eaton sneered, abandoning the pretence. "They wouldn't do that."

"Are you saying members of the council belong to your society too?" Kane's tone was light, but his posture stiffened.

The older man hesitated. "No."

"Then they are under the influence of someone who belongs to your organisation? Danielle, perhaps?"

"She wouldn't bother with the likes of them," he huffed.

"Who would?" I asked, but he paled and shook his head.

"I can't say."

His reaction was closer to that of Mr Spencer's. Whoever this mage was, he was able to frighten grown men. "Are Danielle and this mystery mage in it together?" Kane asked.

"No! She loves me." Kane snorted and Mr Eaton's face hardened. "Just because you couldn't keep her doesn't mean other men can't."

Kane's hand tightened around the fork he was holding, so I hastened to open my phone and pull out the search I'd done previous evening. I showed Mr Eaton the photo of Danielle and Mr Spencer.

"Is this the mystery mage?"

Hexing the Ex

Kane had said Mr Spencer wasn't a mage, but he could've been mistaken. I'd rather be sure. But Mr Eaton's mouth curled in disdain.

"No, he's one of the dupes."

I pushed the phone closer. "He says they've been dating for months."

He wasn't surprised or impressed. "She's just pretending to lure him into our society."

"Are you sure?" I goaded. "He looks very much in love. And she trusted him with the special task of attacking Mr Kane."

Mr Eaton huffed. "She had nothing to do with it."

"It was the other mage, then?" But I figured it out before he could answer. "It was you. You sent him to kill Kane. You thought to get rid of two rivals at one stroke. Spencer kills Kane and then you turn him in to the police."

It made more sense than any of the motives we'd come up with so far.

Anger flashed on his face. "It was a good plan too. But the fool missed, even though he swore he was a brilliant archer. And the arrows were spelled to hit the curse. Yet here you are." He gestured at Kane. He must have been nearby witnessing it to know Spencer had tried.

I nodded. "That's because Kane isn't the one cursed. I am."

The stunned look on his face was almost comical. "What? Danielle wouldn't make such a mistake."

"She didn't," Kane said calmly, as if we hadn't figured it out only that morning. "She knew exactly what she was doing. She made Phoebe trigger the curse so Phoebe would curse me."

I glared at Mr Eaton. "It wasn't Kane you tried to kill. It was me."

Kane leaned closer to him over the table. "So tell me, why I shouldn't strip you of your magic?"

Mr Eaton paled. "You wouldn't do that."

"You used magic to try to kill someone. A human, no less," Kane said remorselessly. "Losing magic is an automatic consequence."

"No, I didn't mean to kill you, just to scare you," the man pleaded, pulling back. Kane followed, leaning over the table.

"You spelled the arrows. Give me one good reason why I should let you keep your magic."

"I…" Mr Eaton slumped, looking forlorn.

"Where did Danielle get the curse?" Kane pressed on. The change of topic fazed Mr Eaton, who frowned.

"France. She lived there after you divorced."

Kane sat back down. "And why did you think it would be effective against me?"

The other man sneered, revelling in his upper hand. "Because the curse isn't what you believe it is. The person who triggers the curse believes himself to be immune, but there's a twist. Every curse you make returns to you. You're basically cursing yourself."

~ ~ ~

I WAS STILL SHIVERING in shock when we returned to the street, the sunshiny day not enough to warm me up again. I was cursed—for real.

Kane led me wordlessly to the Victoria Tower Gardens on the west side of the palace. It was full of people enjoying al fresco lunch, but we managed to find a bench overlooking the river for ourselves.

Hexing the Ex

"I should've realised the curse was too benign to be what we believed," I said, fighting tears.

He wrapped an arm around my shoulder and pulled me against his side. If I hadn't been in shock already, it would've pushed me over the edge. Now I just let him console me.

"It's hardly your fault," he assured me. "I've been studying magic my whole life and it didn't even occur to me. Curses aren't exactly commonplace anymore."

"There must be something I can do."

I could finally appreciate Ashley's anger. It was frightening to be at the mercy of something so out of one's control.

"We'll make Danielle break the curse before they return to you. Let us see, how many people have you cursed and what kind of curses did you put on them?"

I counted with my fingers. "First one was Troy. I wished him interesting times."

His mouth quirked. "So you should expect interesting times in return."

I shot him a sideways look. "You mean more interesting than being shot with an arrow and almost getting eaten by a hellhound?"

"Good point," he grimaced. "Maybe that curse has already returned to you. What else?"

I held another finger. "I hoped that Ashley wouldn't get hurt at work. And now she's unable to do her job."

His brow furrowed. "I don't see how that would apply to our antiques shop, but these things are unpredictable."

I counted another finger. "I wished my former roommate all the best."

He pulled back. "And the curse interpreted that as a hex?"

"Yes. Giselle said it's because few people can handle a sudden burst of good luck."

He nodded. "True. We'll see how you'll handle it when the time comes."

"I could use a bit of luck right now," I sighed. "And the last one was Monsieur André, who I asked to make up his mind already. The curse reacted to that with making him a more efficient person."

"That's useful for an assistant," Kane teased me, and I tried to smile.

"I guess. I'm just glad I stopped there. It's really difficult not to make wishes. I could've caused real damage."

I shivered when I remembered the temptations I'd had so far.

"So how do we proceed?"

He frowned and I braced for being brushed off. "I have to contact the members of the council. Tony has to face the consequences of his actions and I can't punish him alone."

"Is that a priority?"

"It is to the mage community. And there's the mystery mage that has to be dealt with too. If it's not anyone from the council, unless Tony was lying, I have a large pool to investigate."

"But Danielle will find out."

He spread his arms. "It can't be helped. I need other mages to help me deal with her. If she's a warlock, she's too powerful for me alone."

He said it casually, as if talking about a stranger, but his jaw tightened. This really hurt him.

"Maybe the mystery mage running the society is the warlock?" I said, but he didn't look convinced.

"They aren't exactly common. And they wouldn't be part of our community."

"Mr Eaton didn't say he was," I reminded him.

"I would've been told about him already."

"Not if everyone is as afraid of him as Mr Spencer and Mr Eaton are."

He looked puzzled. "I can't imagine who that would be…"

We sat in silence for a few moments. I don't know what he was thinking, but my mind was filled with the curse.

"If we have to kill the caster to break the curse, will you be able to do it?"

His face turned into a mask. "I don't know. It's not exactly something I've had to contemplate before. It's not uncommon for a mage to have to kill demons, but I haven't done that. And I didn't become homicidal even after my divorce, and I was furious with Danielle," he added with a small self-deprecating smirk.

"Maybe you should consider outsourcing it," I suggested, marvelling at the ease of it. We were talking about a human being—or whatever she was now. "I bet Ashley would be willing, if only to be free of the curse."

He shook his head. "I'd like death to be the last course of action. There is a legal procedure against warlocks that should be followed. And I need the council for it."

"So the first course of action would be to find out if she really is a warlock."

His mouth tightened. "Hellhounds don't lie."

"But surely a warlock would have a better scheme going on than blackmailing the rich and famous?" According to Mr Eaton, that was pretty much their whole operation—at least as far as he knew.

"Who knows what's going on in her head," he said, sounding surprisingly bitter. He stood up abruptly. "I'd best get going if I want to visit every council member today. Can you get home all right?"

I rose too. "Home? What about work? It's barely past midday yet."

"It'll hold a day. Go home and rest. Maybe I can rally the council against Danielle and we can get the curse broken in no time."

We returned to the street together, where he hailed a cab. "I can give you a lift, if you like," he said as he opened the door.

"That's all right," I assured him. "Westminster Station is nearby. I can take the Circle Line straight to home."

He left and I ambled towards the station at the other end of Westminster Palace. But when I reached the entrance I didn't want to go in. The day was beautiful, and it would be sweltering in the tube. It was only three miles to home and I was wearing sensible sandals. I could walk. Exercise would do me good, and it would clear my head too. I could even take the scenic route along the river where it would be cooler.

My mind made up, I returned to the street. But to my utter surprise, instead of turning towards Westminster Bridge and the Thames, I chose the opposite direction. The one that led to Hyde Park and the Westbourne Hotel.

Eighteen

ACCORDING TO THE MAP ON my phone, it was a little over two mile walk to Hyde Park. The day was hot, but the route took me through St James's Park and Green Park, where it was slightly cooler in the shade. The scenery was pleasant, and I took my time strolling, pausing once to buy ice cream and water. Nonetheless, I was a bit sweaty and rumpled by the time I reached my destination an hour later.

The Westbourne Hotel was a Victorian redbrick and limestone edifice wedged between modern monstrosities, with an ornamental façade and a view to Hyde Park. It had started its life as a gentlemen's club in the 1880s, but it was already operating as a hotel at the turn of the twentieth century. Five stars, with prices starting from 750 pounds a night. All this I'd learned the previous night when I'd searched for Danielle Mercer.

And now that I was here, I had no idea why I'd come. Blame it on the curse—or the shocking truth about it.

I took a seat on a bench in the park and studied the hotel in indecision. It was a perfectly normal place of business and I couldn't learn anything useful about

Danielle by going in. But if I didn't go in, the walk would've been for nothing.

Reaching a decision, I took out a mirror and brush from my bag and fixed my hair, and then added some lipstick too for further measure. My green silk dress I was wearing again today was by a brand designer, and even though it was dusty after my walk, I wouldn't stand out in it among the fancy hotel guests. Satisfied with my looks, I crossed the street and headed resolutely to the hotel entrance.

A doorman, who had to be sweltering in his long red coat, opened the door for me. "Welcome. Will madam be staying at the hotel?"

I smiled and tried to look like I belonged. I'd often stayed in luxury hotels with my parents, but without them I felt like an impostor. "I hoped to have afternoon tea. Do you serve it?"

"Naturally. Indoors or out?"

Outdoors sounded lovely, so I followed a bellboy through the marble-inlaid lobby to a lounge bar behind the reception, where glass doors were open to a strip of verdant lawn that barely fit between the houses. Several small tables were placed in the shade on a narrow patio by the windows.

The bellboy helped me to a seat at the only available table and a waiter appeared to take my order. There was no menu for me to peruse and no price list. If you had to ask for the price, you couldn't afford it.

I probably wouldn't be able to afford it, what with the renovation expenses looming in my near future, but I'd worry about that later.

I didn't have long to wait for the tea to arrive. To my bafflement, the waiter set the table for two with fine china, and brought some scones too, in addition to the sandwiches I'd ordered.

"I'm sorry, I don't think this is my order," I pointed out, but he only smiled politely.

"The additions were made by your host, madam."

"My what?"

"Me," a woman's voice, low and velvet smooth, stated behind me. I'd never heard it before, but I immediately knew who it belonged to. Danielle Mercer.

My entire body stiffened, and sweat that had nothing to do with the heat began to trickle down my spine. I watched in dismay as she took a seat opposite me. She looked as powerful as the previous night, in a red linen sheath dress, her makeup a bit stronger today and with pearls adorning her throat and ears. How had she known I was here?

The waiter poured us tea, enquired my preferences but not hers, indicating he knew them well, and offered the sandwich plate to me. I took one, even though my mouth had turned to sawdust and I wouldn't be able to eat anything.

"This is nice," Danielle said the moment the waiter had left, as if this was a social call. "We should've done this sooner."

"We don't actually know one another," I managed to say, sounding astoundingly calm, considering how fazed I was. Once again, Mother's teachings about society came to my help, specifically those about entertaining people you didn't like without letting them know. My hand didn't even shake when I lifted the teacup to my mouth, as if I were perfectly relaxed.

I have no idea what the tea tasted like though, and I may have burned my tongue.

"Come now, I'm sure Archie has told you everything about me," she said, amused. She had a beautiful smile, but all I could think of was that she called him Archie. I guess Archibald would've killed the mood in bed.

A sudden image of Kane in bed made me almost forget what we were talking about and I had to struggle to answer. "I didn't even know he'd been married until yesterday."

Her eyes hardened, the gesture minute but clear, before she shook it off. "Apparently you're not important to him, then."

If she thought that was a barb, she was mistaken. Kane and I had a purely professional relationship. "That's right."

I had no idea what to say to her, so I took a bite of my cucumber sandwich instead, hoping she would tell me why she was here. Then again, I didn't even know why I was here.

"He probably hasn't told you about his other life either?" Her challenge was wasted on me. I wasn't here to fight over Kane.

"Magic?" I guessed. "It's a bit difficult to hide that you're a mage when your employee is cursed."

"And how is the curse going?" she asked, taking a sip of her tea.

This time she managed to startle me. I hadn't expected her to admit to sending it. But I only shrugged.

"I was almost killed twice yesterday, so I'd say it's going strong."

She smiled, amused, as if the curse was a joke to her. "Who did you hex for such feedback? You do know about the feedback loop, don't you?"

Hexing the Ex

"Yes. Mr Eaton told us." I had the satisfaction of seeing her mouth tighten. "And I cursed my ex. So I guess that makes two of us." I studied her over the rim of my teacup as I took a sip.

The corner of her mouth curled. "Hexing the ex. How predictable. Surely you don't think that's what this is all about?"

I had no idea what this was about, but I only sneered in return. "Good. Because I didn't curse yours. If you want to harm him, you should take a leaf out of your boyfriend's book and try to make your other boyfriend kill him."

She straightened, dismayed. "What on earth are you talking about?"

"Mr Eaton didn't tell you?"

I knew he wouldn't have contacted her after our visit, because Kane had put a spell on him that prevented him from blabbing, but he might have boasted about it before.

"He sent Mr Spencer with spelled arrows to shoot Kane. Only, he spelled them to hit the person with the curse, and that would be me. I guess you should've told him about the real plan."

Her face tightened with anger. "That idiot. Now Archie has no choice but to strip him off his magic."

"He's preparing for it as we speak. Your little plot is unravelling," I goaded, but she gathered herself and didn't rise to my bait.

"If you think this affects me in any way, you're sorely mistaken."

I made a dismissing gesture with my hand. "I don't really care what you're up to. I only need you to break the curse."

She cocked one of her nicely shaped eyebrows. "Why would I do that?"

"What use is it to you anymore? Kane didn't trigger the curse, so he won't suffer the consequences, and I'm not about to curse anyone again."

"Maybe it amuses me to keep it going…"

My anger flared, banishing the last effects of the thrall I'd been under ever since she showed up, no magic involved. "In that case, we have to seek alternative methods for removing it."

"The only other method is to kill me," she drawled. I shrugged one shoulder, and she sneered. "Archie would never consent to it."

"He doesn't need to know." I met her eyes squarely. She let her gaze sweep slowly up and down me.

"And who would take me down? You?"

I wasn't intimidated by her scorn. "I have friends who are more than capable of dealing with you. After all, we killed your hellhound last night."

She turned deathly pale and the teacup almost fell from her suddenly limp hand. "What hellhound?"

"The one that was guarding your house?"

"It wasn't mine."

I smirked. "What, someone else's hellhound just happened to be in your garden to attack us while yours was nicely tucked by the fireplace the whole evening?"

"I am not a warlock! I can't summon hellhounds." She looked almost sincere in her anger.

"Whose beast was it, then?"

She glanced aside. "I … have a powerful enemy."

I gave her a slow look. "An enemy who decided to help you by getting rid of the people snooping around your house?"

"Of course not," she huffed. "He sent the beast to kill me."

"Why?"

She bit her lip, the gesture oddly vulnerable for a woman as powerful as her. "I stole the curse statuette from him," she confessed. My mouth dropped open.

"And he wants it back badly enough to kill you? With a hellhound." She nodded. "And it attacked us instead?"

If she was telling the truth, the curse had definitely bounced back to me; the chain of events was too unbelievable otherwise.

"Yes." Colour returned to her face. "You shouldn't have been snooping."

"Of course we should have. You cursed me. And the way I see it, we saved your life." My self-confidence returned. "And I know exactly how you can repay. Remove the curse."

But she had managed to get over her shock. "No."

"It's the only way you'll come out of this alive," I pleaded, leaning closer to her. "It's the same to me who kills you, us or your enemy. Either way, I'll be freed from the curse."

She crossed her arms over her chest and studied me. "Is that supposed to be a threat? I might defeat my enemy just as well."

"Provided that you'll still have your magic," I countered. "Kane believes you're a warlock and is preparing to strip you of it. How long will you survive against your warlock enemy once it's gone?"

Anger flashed in her eyes. "Fine. I'll break the curse. But not before you tell him I'm not a warlock."

I nodded magnanimously. "I can do that. Whether he'll believe me is another thing entirely."

"I suggest you try really hard to convince him."

I took a scone and broke a piece, taking time putting jam and clotted cream on it. "It would help if I could tell him something concrete about your enemy," I said, taking a bite. Really good.

"That's none of his concern."

"Is the warlock the true mastermind behind your secret society?"

Her face tightened with fear. The warlock hadn't scared her nearly as much. "No, he's not a warlock. Don't worry about him either. Just make sure Archie doesn't come after me."

"Fine," I echoed her words. "How do we proceed?"

She drummed her red nails against the table as she thought. I'd finished the scone before she spoke.

"I need the statuette and a safe place to perform the ritual."

I gave her a slow look. "Kane will never let you have it."

"The curse can't be broken without the statuette." She shrugged. "But if he wants to supervise, he can attend. We can do it in the gallery. It has enough space for the ritual. There's a full moon on Thursday. That's the most optimal night for it."

"Thursday isn't good for us," I found myself saying, and she smirked.

"What, you have better things to do than removing the curse?"

"We have a gallery opening that night."

She rolled her eyes. "We'll do it after it ends. Midnight works fine."

"Very well, then," I said, nodding. "I'll see you at midnight on Thursday. Or you can come to the opening."

"Thank you, I shall. And you'll stop Archie from coming after me?"

"I will."

I'd got what I wanted here. It was time for me to leave before I—or the curse—ruined it. "Thank you for the tea," I said, getting up. Without a glance back, I walked through the hotel and out of the front door with legs that held, amazingly enough.

That went well.

Nineteen

"I CAN GET THE CURSE LIFTED on Thursday!" I announced the moment I entered the kitchen at home. I was in a brilliant mood. I'd taken initiative and I'd been successful. Danielle might hedge later, but it didn't lessen my achievement now.

Giselle and Ashley were making apple jam and the entire place was filled with a thick, sugary scent that made my mouth water. "That's wonderful news," Giselle said warmly, glancing at me from where she was standing at the stove. "How did you manage that?"

I spread my arms like an actor waiting for applause. "I went to see Danielle Mercer and asked."

"You did what?" they exclaimed in unison, neither of them looking like they would praise me for my brilliance.

Ashley shook her head. She was sterilising jam jars and lids in boiling water, which had to be an accident-prone job, yet the curse let her do it. It really was very specific. "She tried to kill you last night and you went back?"

I took a seat at the table and picked up Griselda, who was pushing against my legs. She at least appreciated me. "I went to the hotel. I figured she couldn't kill me there.

But I had no intention of seeing her. I was having tea and she showed up."

"Just like that?" Giselle asked incredulous. "How does she even know who you are?"

I'd wondered that myself. More to the point, how had she noticed me come to the hotel? Had she sensed the curse?

"I think she's kept a close eye on Kane. He and I figured out that I was actually the intended recipient of the curse."

Giselle almost dropped her ladle in surprise. "Why would she curse you?"

"So that I would trigger it and curse him. But that's not all." They halted what they were doing to look at me. "We learned today that the curse has a feedback loop. Every curse that I've made will return to me. I think she meant for me to suffer too. I think she thought I'm having an affair with Kane."

Even now the notion made me roll my eyes so hard it hurt. Ashley snorted. "Sounds like someone's not over her divorce."

"Exactly, although she claimed she has a bigger plan than petty revenge."

"What did Archibald say?" Giselle asked. I grimaced, my exuberant mood sobering a little.

"He doesn't know yet that I went to her. But I have to tell him that Danielle isn't a warlock."

She gave me a slow look. "How would you know?"

"She told me." She huffed and I lifted my hands. "Even if she lied, that was the stipulation she made for removing the curse."

Ashley looked incredulous. "Where did the hellhound come from, then? I have scars to prove that it was very real."

The mention of hellhound made Griselda hiss as if she'd understood Ashley, and I petted her to calm her down. "She claims that she has a warlock enemy who sent the hellhound to kill her."

"The very night you were there to snoop on her?" Ashley asked the same question I had. "Why?"

"She stole the curse statuette from him."

"Well, that was stupid," she stated. Then she frowned. "So it could be the hellhound sensed the curse in you and came after you on purpose."

My stomach tightened painfully. "Or it could be the first curse looping back to me. I promised Troy interesting times, and people tried to kill me twice yesterday."

Ashley grinned as she lifted jars out of the boiling water to cool on a rack. "I can't wait to see how my curse will hit you."

I shook my head. "There's no telling. I think I was successful with Danielle today, because I wished all the best to Nick. You can't risk yourself at work, but here you are burning yourself with boiling water. And it didn't try to stop you last night with the hellhound, and the risk had to be greater."

"I don't know…" she drawled. "It was a small hellhound."

"Small?" I shrieked, startling Griselda, who jumped down and began to clean herself indignantly. "It was the size of a pony."

"I've seen bigger."

Giselle looked worried. "Who sent it, then, if it wasn't Danielle?"

I threw up my arms, frustrated. "She wouldn't tell."

"But she agreed to lift the curse, just like that?" She began to fill the jars with jam, giving me a side-eye.

I grimaced. "I may have threatened to kill her."

"Archibald will never consent to that."

"He doesn't need to know," I demurred, though I had no idea how we would hide it from him. "But I promised him we'll try peacefully first."

"When will you do it?" Ashley asked. "I can be there as an incentive."

I smiled gratefully. I'd hoped she would offer. "Thursday night, at the gallery. Provided I can convince Kane to agree to it."

"He will. She's his ex-wife, after all," Giselle assured me. "He would never want to hurt her."

I sighed. "I hope it won't come to that." Because if it did, he would never forgive me. "But one way or another, the curse will break on Thursday."

Footsteps approaching from the stairs interrupted us. To my amazement, Nick entered the kitchen. He was dressed more neatly than I'd seen in ages, in new jeans and a slim-fit paisley shirt that had to be his girlfriend's purchases. His hair was an artful mess instead of a dirty one, his face was cleanly shaven, and his eyes were clear. Moving in with Betty had definitely been good for him.

A bright smile spread on his face when he spotted me. "I'm so glad you're home, because I have such good news to tell you," he gushed. "I've been given a role in a big budget American film. Can you believe my luck?"

Hexing the Ex

My stomach tightened in dismay, but I hid my reaction by rising to hug him. "That is wonderful news. I didn't even know you've been auditioning to films."

"I haven't. A casting director saw my play yesterday. And I wasn't even supposed to be on stage. I'm only an understudy, but the lead actor had food poisoning. She approached me after the performance and invited me to audition for the role this morning. They just called and I got the role." His eyes were shining with happiness. "We start shooting on Monday."

"Monday?" I exclaimed, hoping he didn't hear the horror in my voice.

"I know it's fast, but I'm actually a replacement. They had everything ready for another guy, but he broke his leg yesterday, so they had to find a new one in a hurry. And they found me! Soon you can say you're friends with Nick Tanner, the film star."

He finally paused for long enough to look around. He flashed a smile at Giselle and then took in Ashley. "Wow. You look amazing," he said with an appreciative tone. "Have you thought a career in films? Women your size aren't exactly common."

She gave him a bemused look. "What would I play, an amazon?"

"You'd be great as one," he assured her.

He stayed for an hour, drinking Giselle's tea, gushing about the film and how this might be the big break he had been waiting for. I listened in growing upset, trying to look like I was happy for him. And I was. But I was also terrified.

"What shall I do now?" I moaned after he had left. I slumped over the table and buried my face in my outstretched arms. "I can't break the curse now. He'll be devastated if he loses this chance."

Ashley frowned. "You have to have it lifted. I need to go back to work."

I gave her a pleading look. "Couldn't it wait a little? A couple of weeks, maybe? To give him a chance to make an impression. Then he could take it from there on his own."

Giselle patted me on the shoulder. "Maybe the curse merely realigned the world to give him this chance, but his skill is his own."

"I guess…"

"So I suggest you call Archibald before he dashes in to capture Danielle and ruins everything."

It was easier said than done, because he wouldn't answer his phone. "He must have forgotten his mobile in the office again." Although a vague recollection of him looking for it before we left made me doubt it.

"He still has a landline at home," Giselle said. "Try there."

But he wouldn't answer at home either. I tried not to worry. "He's probably still meeting with the members of the council."

I settled down to help Giselle and Ashley with the jam. My job was to glue printed labels on the jars. Giselle sold her jams at a farmer's market and in her shop, so it had to be done carefully. I tried calling Kane again every once in a while, but he still wouldn't answer. The moment the last label was on, I got up.

"I'm going to change and head to the office to see if he left his phone there after all. Then I'll try his home."

"Good idea," Giselle said. "Ashley can go with you. Be back by dinner."

I nodded, not wanting to think about why I would need Ashley for running such a basic errand.

~ ~ ~

THE EARLY EVENING RUSH was at its worst and it took forever to get to the shop. We would probably have made it faster by the tube, but Ashley wanted to drive. "I'm not much for the tube," she said.

"Is it being underground that bothers you?"

"Nah. Just too many people. It's a wolf thing."

I turned to her, full of curiosity. "So how did you become a werewolf?" I absolutely had to ask. "Or is it too traumatic to speak about?"

She shot me an amused look. "I was born one."

"What? I thought you had to be bitten."

She made a small wavy gesture with her hand that was resting on the gear lever. "Well, there's biting involved when a person is old enough to undertake the change. But like with mages, it's genetic."

"And vampires?" I couldn't believe I was asking these questions as if it was a perfectly normal conversation.

"Probably, though I don't know how those fuckers handle the transformation."

"I guess I'll ask Luca."

We lucked out with parking and were soon outside the antiques shop. "I've never been here," Ashley noted, looking curiously though the window into the dark shop. "I'm not much for arts and antiques."

"They've been my passion since I was a little," I told her.

"I've always wanted to be a firefighter like my Dad."

I felt bad for making her work life impossible for her. But we'd soon correct that.

I unlocked the side door that led upstairs and made to enter—only to bounce back. "What the heck?" I tried again, but it was as if the entrance was blocked by an invisible wall. "I can't get in."

Ashley frowned and stepped over the threshold without trouble. "There's nothing there."

I tried again and was blocked again. "Quick, turn off the alarm," I said, since it would be triggered within moments of someone entering.

She reached for the alarm to deactivate it and halted. "The alarm's been triggered."

"Someone's broken in?" My stomach tightened painfully. "Do you think they're still in here?" I asked in a low voice. She shot me a sideways glance.

"Might be why you can't get in." She noticed my baffled look and grinned. "The curse prevents you from getting hurt at work."

"Bugger." I tried to read the alarm display from where I stood. "It's the office. The safe is there."

"I'll go look."

She hurried silently up, then paused at the landing and took a sniff. "There's no one here anymore."

Her words released the curse and the barrier broke. I'd been leaning against it and almost fell on my face. I stumbled after her.

"Was it Danielle?" I wouldn't put it past her to steal the statuette so that she wouldn't have to break the curse.

"No. It smells like demon."

"Demon?" I shrieked, jumping backwards as if one were attacking me. If a hellhound had been bad, demons had to be worse. But she brushed my fear aside.

"Warlocks summon lower-level demons like they do hellhounds. They're bound to their summoner and can only do their bidding."

Since nothing was amiss in the small lobby where my desk was, I went straight to Kane's office and the safe there. If it had been opened, it didn't show any signs of it. I looked around, but nothing seemed to be disturbed in the office either. Kane's mobile wasn't on his desk either, I noted in passing. So why wasn't he answering it?

Ashley sniffed at the safe. "The demon has touched this, but hasn't tried to open it."

"Well, that's good. But why?"

She shook her head. "Maybe it works for the warlock who is after the statuette and came here to fetch it. It could probably sense it isn't in here."

I didn't like it. "How did it know it was sent to us in the first place? Have they captured Danielle? Or are they guessing because she knows Kane?" My stomach tightened painfully.

"They'll go after him next!"

Ashley took me by the arm and pulled me after her. "We have to hurry. The trace here is already cold."

Twenty

IT WAS ONLY A TWENTY-MINUTE DRIVE to Belgravia on the south side of Hyde Park even in rush hour traffic, and Ashley utilised every shortcut she could think of to make it even faster.

Kane lived in the mews behind Eaton Place, a row of modern converts of the old stables and carriage houses of the Regency terraces. They were smallish, compact houses with a garage on the ground level and living quarters above, and with astronomical asking prices due to their popularity.

Parking in the courtyard outside the mews was for residents only, so we left the car on the street and hurried to his house on foot. Kane's Jag was parked sideways in front of his two-bay garage, blocking both doors. If the demon had come here, it had caught him at home.

"The front door is open," Ashley said in a low voice that instantly made me tense.

"Maybe he forgot?" I said hopefully.

"Not bloody likely," she growled, the sound making the small hairs on my neck stand up in fear.

She pushed the door silently open, peeked in, and took a good sniff. Her face furrowed in fury. I was sure she would shift into a wolf, but she dashed up the stairs as silently as a wolf would despite her size, leaving me to follow more clumsily.

The stairs ended at an open-plan kitchen and living room that was primarily done in mid-century Danish modern furniture, all light brown wood and white upholstery. Colour splashes came from red pillows and a genuine Persian rug. The walls were covered with modern art.

All this I noticed in passing. My attention was taken by Ashley, who had tackled a small man in tweed on the floor and was holding him in a chokehold, her long legs wrapped around him so that he couldn't move. But that wasn't the worst of it.

Kane was lying on his back on a long and narrow coffee table, his hands tied together under the table in what had to be a really uncomfortable position. His head was hanging over the top and his ankles were tied to the legs of the table, forcing his legs to bend rather sharply backwards in the knees. Dried blood marred his temple. He was naked except for black boxer briefs, which would've been an interesting sight if there hadn't been burn marks on his torso.

I exclaimed in horror and rushed to release him. He was conscious and furious, the snarl on his face almost as feral as Ashley's.

"Hurry," he commanded, rather unnecessarily, but my fingers were useless against the tight knots around his wrists. "There's a knife in the kitchen."

Getting up, I dashed to the kitchen island that divided the space, past the still struggling Ashley and the intruder, and fetched a knife. Soon I had Kane's hands freed and I helped him to sit up.

Hexing the Ex

"Carefully. You've been hit in the head."

"I've had time to recover from that," he growled. With an elaborate gesture of his fingers, the bindings around his legs fell away and he rose up, only to drop heavily back down again.

"Okay, maybe I need a minute."

"Want me to kill this demon?" Ashley growled.

Kane shook his head, which made him wince in pain. "No, I need to find out who sent him. It's the second time he's come after me, though he wasn't quite this violent before."

I took a closer look at the man too. "That's a demon? He's the one you attacked behind the magic shop," I exclaimed. "I thought he died."

Kane shot me a dismayed look. "I don't kill people, not even demons. I stunned him and he returned to his realm." Then he frowned. "How did you know about the attack anyway?"

"I witnessed it," I confessed.

"And you didn't say anything?"

I grimaced apologetically. "I wasn't entirely sure it was you at the time." In fact, I'd convinced myself it hadn't been. "So who sent him?"

"I thought it was my competitor back then, but I don't think that's the case anymore."

He pushed up again, and this time his legs held. He walked to the pair struggling on the floor and made a series of gestures with his hands that immobilized the attacker.

"You can let go now," he said to Ashley, who pulled away and rose up, adjusting her clothes.

"Who do you work for?" Kane demanded. "And why do you want the statuette?"

The man—demon?—only snarled in answer.

"Who summoned you?" he demanded again.

My mind was busy working out the possible scenarios, and settled on what seemed most likely. I halted Kane by placing a hand on his—bare—arm, and leaned closer to the man/demon.

"Do you work for a warlock whose hellhound was killed last night?"

"What?" Kane bellowed, but I ignored him, my attention on the demon whose face distorted in anger.

"You didn't have to kill it."

"So you do work for him. Why does he want to kill Danielle?"

"The bitch stole his curse statuette. And then she sent it to him." He spat at Kane.

I nodded. Then I turned to Kane. "I think I know what's going on. Banish him to his realm, or whatever. We need to move."

~ ~ ~

THERE ARE SOME THINGS that an employee shouldn't see, and one is their boss in his underwear, no matter how fine his surprisingly sculpted body or how tight the buttocks in his boxer briefs. Nonetheless, I couldn't help sighing a little when he disappeared into his bedroom at the back of the house to put on some clothes.

Ashley nodded, hearing me. "He's a bit puny, but nice to look at."

"Puny?" I was offended on his behalf. "He has an excellent body."

She tilted her head. "I like my men with more meat on their bones."

"And a bit hairier too?" I guessed, and she grinned.

"At certain times of the month anyway…"

We both laughed, the tension of the past hour releasing.

Kane had covered the burn marks with some sort of magical layer that allowed him to put clothes on without pain. Then we drove to the magic shop so that Giselle could treat the burns properly. I was already so used to their alternative methods of dealing with injuries that I didn't even suggest we pop in the closest A&E first.

During the drive, he told us what had happened. "I came home for a quick change. I'm usually more careful with wards, and always put them back up even for a short visit home, but my mind must have been preoccupied, because I forgot." He frowned. "Or he was really good at unravelling them. Either way, I was in my underwear when he attacked. One blow to the head. I woke up tied on the coffee table. I don't know how long I was out, but judging by how numb my arms were, it was quite a long time. And then he began his forceful questioning."

The thought of him being tortured made me shudder.

"He wanted to know where I'd hidden the curse statuette. If you hadn't come when you did, I might have told him too." He looked puzzled. "So how did you happen to arrive so timely?"

"You wouldn't answer your phone, so we went to the office and noticed that the demon had broken in there. We feared he'd come after you and rushed to the rescue."

He smiled warmly. "Thank you."

I smiled in return. "So the statuette wasn't in your home safe either?"

He shot me an admonishing look. "Of course not. Artefacts like that belong to the safekeeping of the council."

Ashley bellowed in laughter. "You are quite something else, Kane, suffering torture for that."

He grinned and blushed lightly. Then he looked at me. "So what is going on? I'm already regretting letting the demon go. He'll only return to annoy me later."

"I'm still piecing it together. I'll tell you when we're all gathered."

Luckily for his patience, the drive went fairly smoothly, and soon enough we were in Giselle's kitchen, where dinner was waiting. I didn't have a chance to speak though, because the moment Giselle learned about Kane's injuries, she refused to proceed until she had treated his burns.

By the time she was done, Amber and Luca had arrived for dinner too. We sat down to eat and I told them what I'd learned that day. Not surprisingly, Kane wasn't happy to hear I'd gone to see Danielle alone.

"Even if the hellhound wasn't hers, which you didn't know going in, we knew she tried to harm you with the curse," he said sternly, his hair billowing again, spurred on by his mood. "It was really reckless of you."

I lifted my hands up in a calming gesture. "I know. But I took a chance and it paid off." I had their attention, so I drew a deep breath and plunged in.

"Danielle stole the curse statuette from a warlock, and came to London with it. Since she's lived here for a while already, I think it took the warlock that long to locate the statuette and come after her. When she realised it, she sent it to Kane for safekeeping. But I think it had to be activated too, so that the warlock couldn't use it in case he got his hands on it. And she likely thought that it would be safer if I was the one triggering it."

"But you said she promised to lift the curse," Ashley pointed out.

"Yes, because I told her she'd die otherwise. Either the warlock kills her and then comes after us to get the statuette, or we kill her. In which case, the warlock will still come after us."

Kane looked dubious. "Are you sure she's not the warlock?"

I shrugged. "She might be a warlock, because why else would she be interested in curses. But the demon definitely wasn't hers, and the hellhound wasn't either, because the demon was upset it was killed, so there's another warlock in play. He wants the statuette and he won't stop until he gets it." I paused to look at everyone at the table. "He isn't above torture and death. So I don't think we can wait until Thursday to have the curse lifted. It has to happen immediately."

"I agree with you, but I will not remove the statuette from the council premises," Kane stated firmly. "That place has wards that'll keep the warlock from finding it."

"Then we'll perform the ritual there."

"Good luck getting Danielle to attend in that case," Amber said, reaching for a pitcher of water and filling her glass. "You'll need to give her great sureties that you're not removing her magic."

Kane put down his utensils. "She still needs to answer for her activities in trying to teach humans magic."

"And she will," Giselle said, patting his arm. "But later. The curse has to come first."

"Fine," he sighed. "I'd best call off the council meeting, so we can have the place to ourselves. Then we'll have to figure out how to lure Danielle to the meeting."

"I can club her unconscious," Ashley suggested.

"I can mesmerise her," Luca said.

Kane lifted his hands up, halting them. "Thank you, but it's time I face my fears and ask her myself. Nicely."

That didn't mean he wanted to do it alone—although he claimed we were there in case the warlock showed up. Amber and Giselle headed to the council house ahead of us to prepare it for the ritual, while the rest of us went to fetch Danielle.

At that time of evening, the streets of her neighbourhood were lined with cars and we had to leave ours further down the street. Everything looked calm, but I was slightly wary as we approached Danielle's house, until Ashely assured us that there were no hellhounds around. She stayed on the street, though, to keep watch, while the rest of us went to Danielle's door.

But Kane hadn't even knocked on it when Ashley called.

"The bitch just drove past me. Get in the car, we have to follow."

Twenty-one

"TAKE HER PLATE NUMBER," Luca ordered as we filed through the narrow gate and hurried to the car. Ashley was already behind the wheel and starting the engine.

"You take it. It's that white Fiat 500 heading past the park."

Before Ashley managed to turn the large car around on the narrow street and drive after her, Danielle's vehicle was already at the end of the street, turning left. I pulled out a map on my phone.

"She could be headed back to the hotel," I said, as she turned east at the next street corner.

"Or my place," Kane said. "It's only a couple of streets away from it."

Or anywhere, really, as the entirety of Central London was in that direction. But then she turned away from the eastbound road that would've taken here there. "North," I noted.

"She can get to Cromwell Road there," Luca said. "It leads to the hotel."

He had opened an app with which he could track Danielle's vehicle based on its plate number. I wasn't sure it was legal for him to have it, but I wasn't about to complain.

She didn't take Cromwell Road either and just continued north at every opportunity. I studied the map. "She's not headed to Holland Park, is she?"

Kane shot me a puzzled look from the front seat. "You think she's going to Spencer's? Surely she knows he's not home?"

I shrugged. "Not necessarily. You prevented him from contacting her. I didn't tell her he's left, and I doubt she's so attached to him she would call him every day. Besides, it was only yesterday evening that he left."

Though it felt much longer.

"But why would she flee us there?" Ashley asked. "That's hardly a safe house."

I perked. "Maybe she doesn't even know we're following her. She couldn't see to her front door from the car, so she wouldn't have noticed us there."

"She's driving really fast though," Luca noted.

"She always does," Kane said dryly.

"Maybe she's worried for Mr Spencer," I suggested. "Maybe she fears the warlock's got him when he doesn't answer his phone."

"That's anticlimactic," Ashley grumbled. "Here I thought I was in a proper car chase."

I was proven right. Five minutes later, Danielle parked her car in Mr Spencer's empty driveway, rushed out, ran up the stairs, and banged on the front door. Ashley pulled over right behind her car, blocking her exit, and Kane and I climbed the stairs after Danielle.

"Joe? Are you there?" she shouted when no one opened the door.

"He's not home," Kane said.

Hexing the Ex

Danielle shrieked in fright, twirled around and launched an energy ball that would've hit Kane squarely in the chest if he hadn't deftly parried it with deflecting magic. It hit the rosebush by the door instead and set it on fire.

She stared at him bewildered, breathing hard. "What the hell, Archie? Why are you here?"

"I'm here to tell you that Mr Spencer isn't home," he said calmly, as if there wasn't a fire burning by his elbow. He made pinching motion with his hand and the fire disappeared.

"How would you know? The warlock could've got him," she said frantically, but Kane was unmoved.

"I sent him to safety yesterday."

"And didn't tell me?" she demanded, pulling herself together.

"Why would I tell you anything?" he asked, irritated, crossing his arms over his chest. "It was you I was trying to protect him from in the first place."

She staggered back, as if he had hit her. "Why would I harm him?"

He leaned closer to her face and looked her straight in the eyes, not buying her upset at all. "He tried to kill Phoebe on your society's orders, so forgive me if I wasn't going to take that chance."

"I didn't order him to attack her!"

"Says you," he countered. Mr Eaton had already confessed, but he was so besotted with her he could be taking the blame just as well. Besides, we hadn't known that when we sent Mr Spencer away.

I lifted my hands between them, pushing them apart from each other. "Let's calm down. The most important thing is that Mr Spencer is safe. The warlock hasn't attacked him—unlike Kane."

Danielle paled. "He attacked you?"

"No, he sent his pet demon," he said, grumpily. "And I dealt with it. But we can't wait any longer to break the curse, because they really want that statuette back. Next time you go stealing from warlocks, make sure they don't know where to find you."

She made to answer, but the front door was pulled open just then, startling us all. Kane and Danielle readied energy balls, before they realised who it was.

Troy was standing on the threshold, wearing only a towel around his hips. He had a nice, lean body, but after having witnessed what Kane was hiding under his clothes, it paled in comparison. He studied us, bewildered. Then he spotted me.

"Phoebe? What are you doing here?"

I looked indignant. "Me? What are you…? Wait, didn't we have this conversation already? Your girlfriend isn't home, you know."

"I'm housesitting."

"Right…"

Kane cleared his throat. "I think we'd best go. We have a lot to do tonight."

He took Danielle by the elbow and made to head down the steps, when a young woman wearing a towel that barely covered her impressive assets appeared behind Troy and wrapped herself around him.

"Come back to bed already," she purred.

Troy glanced at us, then her, and then back at us, his eyes growing large in panic. Kane solved his dilemma by wrapping his free arm around mine and walking us down the steps before I could point out that the woman most definitely wasn't Amelia Spencer. Some house-sitter he was.

"That wasn't Amelia," Danielle huffed, indignant, when the door closed behind us.

Ashley was laughing so hard tears were falling down her face. "That's some curse you put on that fucker. The only thing missing here is the girlfriend returning home and catching the two in the act."

I grinned too. "That might happen yet."

She wiped her eyes. "Pity we're breaking the curse today."

"Troy doesn't need a curse to behave like an ass."

Danielle frowned. "I thought we agreed that the curse will be lifted on Thursday when it's the full moon."

"We can't wait," Kane said. "We have everything ready, so you have to come with us to break the curse immediately."

Danielle stiffened and her hand began to curl into a fist in preparation of an energy ball. "I will not let you strip me of my magic!"

"I'm not going to," he assured her. "I just need you to break the curse so that I can hide the statuette for good before the warlock gets his hands on it."

She shot him a suspicious look. "So you believe that I'm not a warlock?"

He shrugged. "That remains to be seen. But for now I'm willing to give you the benefit of the doubt." He opened the back door of Ashley's car. "Hop in. We're driving."

~ ~ ~

IT WAS A SIXTEEN-MILE drive to Thames Ditton, a village south of Hampton Court Park, not far from Hampton

Court Palace, where Henry VIII used to live, but on the south side of the river. It was getting late, so traffic was light and we made the journey in a little over half an hour.

It felt like a decade. If I'd thought the drive with Mr Spencer was awkward, this one made it feel like a country picnic. Danielle was wedged between Luca and me on the back seat, and while it was a spacious seat, her anger made it small.

She and Kane bickered the whole drive like kids—or like a divorced couple who'd never had a chance to normalise their relationship. Most of it had nothing to do with the case at hand, as if they'd just picked up where they'd left.

I'd never seen this side of my boss before—he was usually courteous and quick to calm down—so I watched them in fascination, sharing bemused glances with Luca behind Danielle's back when they began to go through the events of a family Christmas party over a decade ago.

Ashley wasn't amused. She slammed on the brakes, bringing the car to such a sudden stop that I almost hit my head on the seat in front of me, the seatbelt digging painfully into my shoulder.

"If you two don't shut the fuck up right the fuck now, you can fucking walk!" she bellowed, glowering at Kane and Danielle. He gave her a sheepish grimace, but Danielle lifted a haughty brow.

"Who are you to order me about?"

"I'm the one driving, how about that, bitch?"

"She's also the werewolf who killed the hellhound last night, so I'd do what she says," I said to Danielle. She crossed her arms over her chest in a petulant show of temper, but she remained silent for the rest of the drive.

Small mercies. I would've had a million questions about the ritual and my role in it, but I thought it best not to bring them up until we were safely out of the car.

The mage council's headquarters was in an erstwhile priory in a neighbourhood that hosted a pub from the thirteenth century and other old houses. It was a large, rectangular brown-brick that had its current façade from the Georgian era. It lined the courtyard to a rambling Queen Anne style manor that had been converted to an expensive care home for the elderly, and shared its parking lot. Despite the quiet location, it was an oddly public place for a secretive organisation, but Kane told me the council had inherited it from a wealthy mage a century ago.

The place was dark and quiet, and for a moment I thought Giselle and Amber hadn't made it there yet, but that turned out to be an illusion. Inside, the entrance hall was warmly lit, illuminating a gleaming parquet floor and wainscoted walls. Amber was waiting for us.

"Good, you're finally here. What kept you?"

"We had to chase Danielle down," I quipped, causing the woman in question to glare at me.

"How was I supposed to know you were following me?"

Amber cut her off with an impatient wave of her hand. "Never mind. Let's head to the ritual room."

That sounded ominous. My heart was beating fast as I followed Amber and Danielle through a dining room with French windows to the erstwhile chapterhouse of the priory. Old wooden pews lined two walls of the square room, but a modern meeting table and chairs filled the floor too and I guessed that was where the Council of Mages met.

At the other end, a door led to a small closet that had been the vestry of the former chapel on its other side, now full of office supplies. In one corner, a spiral stone staircase led down.

"This place has two floors above ground and we have to go below?" I grumbled to myself, but Kane answered.

"We have a room for rituals upstairs, but this one requires extra wards, so we'll do it here."

My sense of excitement and dread increased with every step down. I imagined a damp dungeon, but was disappointed. The vaulted grey stone ceiling and limestone floor were clean and airy. Racks of wine bottles stood on the wall closest to the stairs, and the rest had been renovated to a rather cosy clubroom. A mahogany bar stood on one side, with large leather recliners and small tables filling most of the space.

They had been pushed to one side to clear the floor for the ritual at the far end. Amber and Giselle had drawn a ritual circle on the limestone floor big enough to fit a couple of people sitting down. Large candles were placed on the compass points.

Amber handed Danielle some chalk. "You draw the rest, since it's your ritual."

Danielle scrunched up her nose. "I'm still not sure this is a good idea."

"You promised," I reminded her.

Ashley growled, showing fangs, and Luca took a threatening step towards Danielle too. Kane halted them.

"It's imperative for your safety," he stated.

Her sneer was bitter. "Like you care."

"Of course I do," he said, relenting a little. "The warlock won't wait for you to remove the curse if he gets his hands on the statuette. He'll simply kill you."

For a moment it looked like she would refuse anyway, but then she took the chalk from Amber. "Fine."

She set out to work under the watchful eyes of three mages, drawing careful lines on the floor.

"That's a rather harsh-looking pattern," Giselle noted, making Danielle roll her eyes.

"That's because it's dark magic. It's not exactly into pretty things."

Once she was done, she removed the candles from the compass points to between them. Amber's brows shot up. "It would never have occurred to me to do that. Where did you learn all this?"

"I spent years studying."

"Why?" Kane demanded.

She gave him a steady look. "You know why. You divorced me for the why."

Kane inhaled, clearly intending to rekindle their fight, so I put a hand on his arm. "Let's get this over with first. You can talk about the finer points of magic later."

"Fine," they both said in a tone that clearly indicated the opposite.

"Now, what should I do?" I asked Danielle.

"I need you to sit inside the circle."

I looked at the pattern on the floor and shuddered. "Are you sure it's safe?"

She sneered. "It hasn't been activated yet." She turned to Kane. "I need the statuette."

He nodded and headed to the other end of the room, disappearing behind the wine racks. I stepped gingerly over the chalk lines and sat on the floor, crossing my legs. The stone was cold under my buttocks and I hoped the ritual wouldn't take long.

Kane returned with the statuette and paused in front of Danielle with it. "You do understand that this won't leave the premises? I don't care what your deal with the warlock is, he can't have it."

"Why do you think I sent it to you in the first place?" she huffed, taking the statuette. She stepped into the circle, placed the totem of swirling snakes between us, and sat down opposite me.

"Now, let's begin."

My companions took places around the circle, making sure she wouldn't be able to get away without breaking the curse. She smirked, but didn't say anything. She just closed her eyes and steadied her breathing. Mine was erratic.

She opened her eyes again and made to speak, when a male voice sounded from the other end of the room.

"What's going on here?"

Twenty-two

WE ALL TURNED TO LOOK. Danielle groaned, aggravated, when she recognised Mr Eaton. He crossed the room to the circle and looked around baffled. Then he noticed the ritual circle.

"Danielle?"

She shot him a disgusted look. If the two were in love like he had claimed, she wasn't feeling it at the moment. "What are you doing here?"

"I came to plead with the council for my case, but no one's here," he said. "What are you doing?"

"We're breaking the curse, what does it look like," she snapped.

He deflated a little. "But … why?"

Kane put a hand on his shoulder. "It's the only way to keep her from being killed by a vindictive warlock."

"I can protect you," Mr Eaton declared, but his chivalric gesture was wasted on Danielle.

"Not bloody likely."

"We'll take the statuette and flee where that horrid warlock can't find us!" Mr Eaton said fervently, as if he hadn't heard what she said. He lunged into the circle, took the statuette and held it close to his chest. "Come on!"

We were all so stunned by his stupid move that no one tried to stop him. Danielle rose up, and I shot her a baffled look. "You're not seriously leaving with him?"

Ashley got her wits together and wrapped her arms tightly around the much smaller Mr Eaton. "He's not leaving anywhere either."

She wrenched the statuette from Mr Eaton and threw it to me. I managed to catch it and a creepy sensation spread from it through my body. Repulsed, I placed it hastily back on the floor.

Danielle smiled, slowly. I thought it was to mock me for my weakness, but then she gestured with her hand—and my body froze.

It was the oddest sensation. I could breathe and move my head, but I couldn't stand up or move any other part of my body. It was as if it wasn't even there. A surge of fear made my heart speed up and my breathing turned shallow.

"What did you do?" Kane demanded. I managed to turn my head far enough to look at him and saw that Danielle had frozen all of us. My friends and Mr Eaton were standing like living statues around the circle. "How is it possible for you to control so many of us at once?"

She sneered. "Like I said, I've been studying." She leaned down and picked up the statuette. "I believe I'm leaving."

"What about me?" Mr Eaton asked, bewildered.

"I'm leaving alone. It's for your own good. All of you."

"But you'll die," I said, desperately. She looked me squarely in the eyes as she straightened.

"I'll take my chances."

"They'd be much better if you removed the curse first," I tried to plead with her, but she shook her head.

"I like the curse just the way it is."

She turned to leave and I racked my brain frantically for how to stop her. I couldn't move—none of us could. I had nothing but words to use and she seemed to be impervious to threats.

And then: clarity. Maybe it was my own ingenuity, maybe it was Monsieur André's curse looping back to me, but I knew exactly what I should do.

"I have to make you want to break the curse, then," I said, halting her. She looked at me over her shoulder with great disdain.

"And how would you do that? Your precious werewolf is immobile and can't kill me, as is the vampire. Your mage friends are unable to spell anything. By the time you're free, I'll be long gone. You've already lost."

My anger flared at her taunt and I inhaled sharply. But instead of trying to calm down, I gathered the anger and moulded into the strongest desire and intention I was capable of. Then I spoke, and my words had power.

"I wish you long life with the first man who tells you he loves you," I said, releasing my will.

The impact of the curse was instant and staggering. Power exploded from the statuette and threw me backwards against the legs of whoever was standing behind me. The last thing I heard before I passed out was Mr Eaton shouting:

"I love you, Danielle. I love you!"

~ ~ ~

I CAME TO ON one of the clubroom sofas. Giselle was sitting by me, wiping my forehead with a damp cloth. She smiled when I opened my eyes.

"Did it work?" I asked, holding my breath until she nodded.

"Yes. You made her break the curse. Well done."

Amber leaned over her shoulder. "How did you come to think of such an odd curse?"

"The feedback from Monsieur André's curse came to my help." I pushed to sit up. My head spun a little, but it settled down fast. "It gave me clarity. I needed a curse with instant repercussions, one that she would find repulsive, but which I could live with in case she refused to break the curse anyway."

I had no one in my life confessing his love to me, but there could be in the future—and hopefully he would be someone I loved in return. I could think of worse curses than spending a long life with a man who loved me.

Unlike Danielle.

"She couldn't get rid of the curse fast enough," Giselle said, shaking her head. "She wouldn't even wait for you to come to and had broken it before we'd properly propped you back in the circle. Tony was devastated. I had to give him one of my special teas so that he would calm down."

I felt bad for him, but he lived in a fantasy of his own making. I looked around. "Where's everybody?"

"Upstairs. Archibald is questioning Danielle, and Ashley and Luca are keeping watch. Tony is sleeping over there." Giselle pointed at a similar leather sofa on the other side of the room. "The curse statuette is safe and secure in a vault behind several wards, one of which will trap whoever tries to remove it, even a warlock."

"Good."

The women helped me up and we headed upstairs, leaving Mr Eaton to sleep. "He'll be safe here," Amber assured me. I wouldn't want to wake up alone in an empty cellar, but at least the place was familiar to him.

We found our people in the chapterhouse. Danielle was secured in one of the chairs by the table, rendered immobile by the same spell she had used on us. Kane was sitting in front of her, asking her questions, and judging by the frustrated look on his face, it wasn't going well. Ashley and Luca were standing at her sides, but they abandoned their post when they spotted me, and came to hug me tightly. I hugged them back, happy to have them in my life.

Kane rose up too. "Are you all right?" He put hands on my shoulders and studied my face for signs of concussion or maybe residues of magic. He didn't find anything alarming, because the lines on his face eased.

"Absolutely," I assured him. "Someone softened my landing."

"That would be me," Luca said with a grin. "I may have bruises."

I resisted the urge to stick my tongue out at him, but he seemed to sense it, because his grin deepened. Danielle was glowering at me.

"That was a really rotten curse."

I couldn't stop the wide smile that spread on my face. "I said I'd force your hand. I figured you wouldn't want to spend the rest of your life with Mr Eaton."

She shuddered. "Not hardly."

Kane squeezed my shoulder. "Any residue from the curse?"

I tried to listen to my body, but I didn't feel any different. "I guess I won't know if it worked until I try making a wish again."

"No!" everyone shouted at once, and I grinned.

"What? Don't you trust Danielle?"

She sneered. "The curse is gone. You can take that to the bank."

I went to her and leaned down to look her in the face. "I wish you would tell us everything about the secret society and the mastermind behind it." I braced for a blackout, but it didn't happen. I shrugged. "I guess you were telling the truth."

"Of course I was," she spat. "I'd kill myself if I had to spend a lifetime with that fool."

I tilted my head. "That would've broken the curse too…"

"Well then, now that we know you're fine, we should go home," Kane said. "It's getting late."

Danielle smirked. "Can't wait to be alone with her, can you?"

He pulled back, looking so stupefied that I had to laugh. "She thinks we're having an affair."

The withering look he shot at his ex-wife would've made a weaker person quake. "I do not get involved with my employees. Don't you know me at all?"

"I know you perfectly," she shot back. "Now, will you let me go or do I have to spend the night in this chair?"

Kane actually looked like he was tempted to leave her there. Then he huffed, disgusted. "Just go. And try to stay out of my life, please."

He motioned with his hand and the invisible restraints holding her disappeared. She stood up and straightened her clothes.

"Gladly."

Without a glance at any of us, she left the room. We followed at a slower pace. I couldn't believe it was over, and so easily. I'd had to suffer another blackout, but hopefully it hadn't caused permanent damage.

Cool night air hit me when I stepped out of the building, refreshing me. Mist was rising from the river, giving the courtyard a suitably eerie look—now that we didn't need such theatrics anymore.

Danielle was standing in the driveway, clicking her phone. We glanced at each other and then Giselle, always the nice one, led our group to her.

"We can give you a lift to your car," she offered.

Danielle didn't even glance up from her phone. "Thank you, but a chauffeur from the hotel will pick me up."

Giselle looked like she would press a bit more, out of politeness. But before she could, the air in front of Danielle shimmered and a small pressure wave pushed us back a step or two.

A tall, leanly muscled man stepped out of thin air. He wore tan trousers and a white shirt with its sleeves rolled up and top buttons open, somewhat disappointingly to his grand entrance; there wasn't even a wizard's robe in sight. He was in his early forties and handsome in a stark way. There was something French about his hooked nose, arrogant sneer, and hint of grey at the temples of his elegantly cut black hair. He wasn't the most handsome man I'd ever seen, but he practically oozed sexiness. My entire body tightened with sudden arousal.

His gaze homed in on Danielle, who was staring at him with her mouth hanging open. He reached his hand to her, and there was something sad in his smile. "Come, *chérie*. It's time to go home." His accent was definitely French.

She studied the hand for a couple of heartbeats. Then she sighed and straightened herself, looking at him squarely. "You're not getting the statuette."

"I don't care about the statuette."

She nodded and took his hand. They stepped into the shimmering portal and disappeared, like they'd never even been here.

It was as if a spell had broken when they were gone. "You saw that too, right?" I asked, not sure if my battered brain hadn't come up with a vivid hallucination of sexy men appearing out of thin air.

"We did," Luca assured me. "Wow."

"Can you guys do that too?" I asked.

"That was a warlock," Amber said, shaking her head. "Only they can move through space like that."

Kane looked shocked. "Was he the one trying to kill her? We'll have to go after her."

I wrapped an arm around his and began to lead him to the cars. "She went with him voluntarily. I don't think things are what we thought they were."

"What you thought, you mean?" he said, shooting a sideways glance at me.

"I didn't have all the facts."

"And what would those be?"

We paused outside the cars, no one going in until they'd heard my latest version of events. But this time I was pretty sure I knew what was going on.

"If I'm not much mistaken, that was the warlock who has been teaching her the darker side of magic. But it wasn't a simple student-teacher relationship, because no one goes to this much trouble for a former student. They were in love. For whatever reason, she left him and took the curse statuette with her. Either she wanted revenge, or she wanted him to come after her. And now he has. And to prove his love for her, he said he didn't care about the statuette."

"But he tried to kill her," Ashley exclaimed.

I shrugged. "That's what she said. But perhaps the hellhound was there to locate her—or the cursed person, aka me."

Kane looked grim. "She could've been fleeing a domestic situation. Warlocks aren't exactly nice people."

"Neither is she," Amber said. "And she's learning to be a warlock too."

"That's death magic," Giselle added. "Abuse is probably part of it."

My stomach tightened. The part of me that had been utterly taken with the raw sexuality he'd emanated couldn't believe he would be abusive, but he was a warlock; he'd killed to become one.

Kane didn't look happy either, but he shook his head. "Nothing we can do to help her now. I tried to talk her out of it when we were married. She went anyway. If she's not strong enough to handle the path she's taken, she'll return eventually."

I gave him a consoling pat on the shoulder. "I'm sure we'll find her again." Then I snorted, amused. "She was wrong, you know."

A wall of questioning faces looked at me.

"This was definitely about hexing the ex."

Epilogue

THE OPENING OF MONSIEUR ANDRÉ'S exhibition was a great success. And that's what he was called again, now that the curse was gone.

Some changes were permanent, however. His greedy boyfriend was still out, he wasn't smoking, and he was wearing black jeans and a black silk shirt without any scarves. It gave me hope that some effects of Nick's curse would linger too, giving him a chance to become a movie star. And even though Ashley had been able to return to work, maybe she would be protected by the curse too.

Kane and I were standing at the gallery door, greeting people coming and going. "I think I can sell at least three paintings tonight," he said, looking satisfied by the turnout.

"That's excellent," I said warmly. Things were back to normal between us too, as if the interlude with curses and magic had never happened. He hadn't brought it up once in the intervening days, and if I hadn't had my housemates with whom to go through the events, I might have thought I'd imagined everything.

Danielle had left London, as I'd learned after I called the hotel and asked for her. "A family emergency is keeping her away for a few days, I'm afraid," her secretary had told me. I had a notion that the emergency would turn into a permanent leave later.

Mr Spencer, having been given a permission to return home, had visited the gallery earlier that day to inquire after Danielle. Kane's spell still prevented him from contacting her directly. It had been my unfortunate duty to inform him that she'd returned to her old boyfriend.

"Laurent Dufort?" he asked sharply, pronouncing the French name beautifully. I recognised the name as the last known owner of the curse statuette—from a century and a half ago. Maybe warlocks truly lived longer.

"I knew it was going to happen sooner or later. A passionate affair like theirs won't just die."

"Do you know why she left him in the first place?" I asked, curious.

He shrugged, looking sad. "I don't know the details. They had a huge fight and she walked away, and then she couldn't swallow her pride to go back."

"So there was nothing … domestic about it?" I asked carefully.

He inhaled sharply. "That he would've hurt her? I don't think so. She would've said something."

I planned to tell that to Kane at first chance so that he could stop worrying about her.

Kane glanced at me. "I'm sorry I haven't been around to help with the opening. I've been busy dealing with the aftermath of breaking Danielle's society."

I smiled. "We managed with Mrs Walsh. So you put an end to it?"

"Yes, thanks to Luca identifying all the attendants. But Tony has disappeared."

My stomach fell. "Voluntarily?"

He grimaced. "I truly hope so. But I fear the mastermind they were so afraid of has done something to him. We still don't know who he is. Finding it out will be my next priority."

I felt sorry for Mr Eaton, but only briefly. He had tried to kill me after all.

We greeted a couple of people coming in and I handed them leaflets about the exhibition. When they were gone, Kane smiled at me.

"The council is pleased with how I handled the situation. I think there won't be any challenges for my position as the leader after all. Smooth sailing from now on."

He walked off to talk with a potential buyer, leaving me to stare after him in dismay.

I'm not one for premonitions, but I think he had just jinxed everything.

Acknowledgements

I would like to thank all the usual suspects: my husband for his unwavering support. My sisters for their comments and encouragement. And my editor for making my book shine. The remaining mistakes are all mine. And last, but not the least, I would like to thank all of you, my wonderful readers. Without you, there wouldn't be these books.

About the Author

SUSANNA SHORE is an independent author of more than twenty books. She writes *Two-Natured London* paranormal romance series about vampires and wolf-shifters that roam London, and *P.I. Tracy Hayes* series of a Brooklyn waitress turned private investigator. She also writes stand-alone thrillers, and contemporary romances with billionaires and the strong women who love them. When she's not writing, she's reading or—should her husband manage to drag her outdoors—taking long walks.

Made in United States
North Haven, CT
20 April 2023